G000130241

Joonie And The Great Harbinger Stampede

Sakura Publishing
PO BOX 1681
Hermitage, PA 16148
www.sakura-publishing.com

Ordering Information:
Quantity sales. Special discounts are available on quantity purchases by corporations, associations, and others. For details, contact the publisher at the address above.

Orders by U.S. trade bookstores and wholesalers. Please contact Sakura Publishing:
Tel: (330) 360-5131; or visit www.sakura-publishing.com.

Printed in the United States of America

First Edition
ISBN-10: 0984678549
ISBN-13: 978-0-9846785-4-9
Book cover and design by Michael King
Book editing by Jason Heller

www.sakura-publishing.com

Printed in the United States of America

14 13 12 11 10 / 10 9 8 7 6 5 4 3 2 1

To Erin -

Thank you so much for all you do around these parts. I am so greatful for the work you did on the Joonie website.

Much love,

JOONIE

AND THE GREAT HARBINGER STAMPEDE

Also Released by Sakura Publishing

Tourettics

Lost Evidents

Fortino

When Heaven Calls

Dump Your Problems!

The Legend of Willow Springs Farm

Stricken Yet Crowned

Did I Really Do My Hair For This?

Defeat Wheat: Your Guide To Eliminating Gluten and Losing Weight

Death of a Black Star

Elvolution

It's Good to Share

The Yearn Parade

The Glass Girl

JOONIE

AND THE GREAT HARBINGER STAMPEDE

a myth by

Daniel Landes

art by

Ravi Zupa

To the Brothers Landes:
breathe & behold

FOREWORD

The best authors nourish the soul. In Dan Landes' case, that nourishment is literal.

Many years ago I began eating at his Denver restaurant WaterCourse Foods, which had just opened. It was a small, humble vegetarian place. That said, WaterCourse was committed—and it still is—to serving food that's far heartier than what people might expect from a meat-free eatery.

But it was more than Dan's food that nourished. Even as WaterCourse grew into the thriving cornerstone of Denver's community that it is now, it had a vibe. It was warm. It was earthy. It was soulful.

And that was all before Ravi Zupa came along.

Ravi is a visual artist from Denver whom Dan commissioned to begin painting murals inside WaterCourse. They were gorgeous. Lavishly detailed, they depicted herds of buffalo, families of rabbits, and other animals coexisting in a prairie setting. On a deeper level, they illustrated the ethic of empathy and sustainability that WaterCourse embodies. But on the surface, they were simply stunning to look at.

Later I came to learn that Ravi's murals weren't conceived as mere wallpaper.

There was a story behind them.

For years Dan has had this story bubbling in the back of his mind. It involves his own grappling with certain questions, some of which have haunted him since childhood. Questions like, how can organisms coexist peacefully? What is the nature of individual self-awareness versus collective identity, and how do beings come to possess it? The future restaurateur in him also wondered about humankind's biblical fall from grace—specifically the role eating played in that fall.

From there, Dan's ideas and Ravi's artwork began to take on a shape of their own. That shape? A book: Joonie and the Great Harbinger Stampede.

As a book, Joonie is a fun, thrilling read. It has an intrepid young hero on a journey of self-discover, brave friends, horrifying villains, and an epic adventure that leaves none unchanged.

But, like the murals in WaterCourse, there's a deeper level.

Joonie is a young, frail rabbit, and he is on a quest. He didn't ask to go on that quest. He has no choice. But along the way, he begins to embrace his destiny. He grows. That growth, though, isn't measured in inches. Its measured in spirit. It's measured in the way Joonie's own consciousness, his own identity, is pitted against the wants and needs of the many.

Animals, Joonie comes to discover, are tribal in nature. That tribalism takes many forms. It can be used for good or for ill. It can be healthy or dysfunctional. Usually it's some combination of these elements. Like an ecosystem, collectives seek their own balance. But what happens when different collectives, different tribes, come in conflict with each other? When there are only so many resources to go around? Does it all boil down to Might Makes Right? Kill Or Be Killed? Is there a more humane path? And in the midst of these species-wide conflicts, how much power—if any—does the individual have? And if?

These are heavy questions. Indeed, long before Dan pondered them, philosophers since the dawn of time have debated them. Joonie doesn't necessarily find the answers, any more than Dan (or the philosophers) do. In fact, Joonie and the Great Harbinger Stampede is far more than a book of ideas. It's a book of action. It's a book of horror. It's a book about Joonie's coming-of-age, during which he confronts the limits of his own instincts and compassion and fear—and then learns how to push beyond them.

That said, it's also a book of great laughter. Like one's headstrong best friend, the porcupine known as Pencilthin is as brave and valiant as he is hilariously foolhardy. Like a Zen master, the character of Grandfather Tortoise speaks in infuriating riddles, with a wry sense of humor concerning even the most frightening aspects of the universe.

And that, at its heart, is what Joonie and the Great Harbinger Stampede is all about. It's about how the big questions and giant forces in the world can be embodied in the smallest beings. It's about the ironies and paradoxes that make life both absurd and rich in wonder.

And it's about nourishment: of the body, of the mind, and of the soul. After all, for as long as I've known Dan and partaken of his food, his friendship, and his wisdom, that's always been his bread and butter.

—*Jason Heller*

The Sun, hearth of affection and life,
pours burning love on the delighted earth.

Arthur Rimbaud

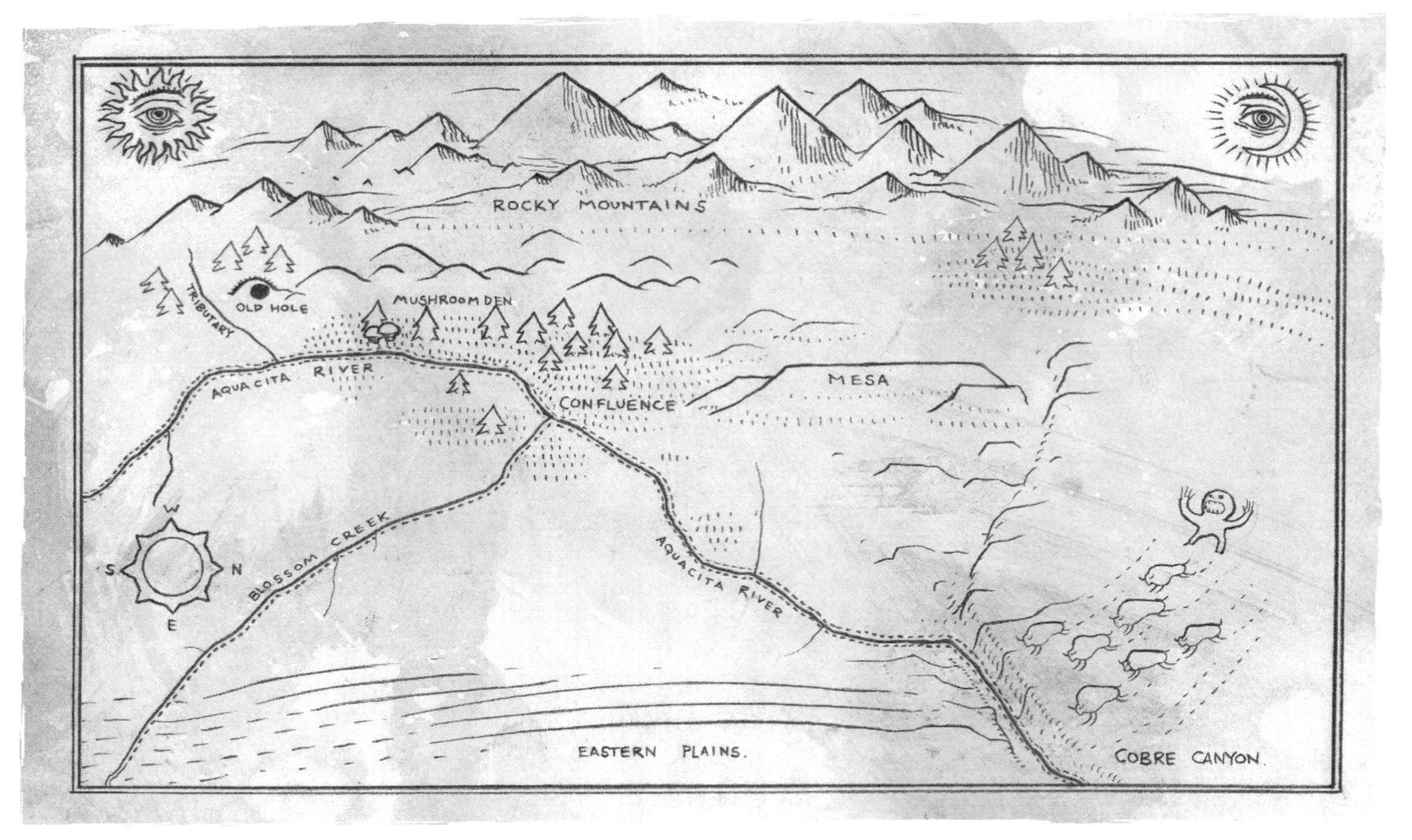
ROCKY MOUNTAINS
TRIBUTARY
OLD HOLE
MUSHROOM DEN
AQUACITA RIVER
CONFLUENCE
MESA
W
S
N
E
BLOSSOM CREEK
AQUACITA RIVER
EASTERN PLAINS.
COBRE CANYON.

PROLOGUE

The First War

She lay in the shade of a tree adorned with fragrant blossoms, watching the clouds drift by. She thought of nothing, and almost nothing thought of her.

The Sun illuminated first her toes and then began a slow promenade up her legs.

In the shade he scratched his head, beheld his fingernails, and gave them a curious sniff. He looked at her and then the tree. He followed her eyes up to the drifting clouds. To him, his fingernails, her, the tree, and the clouds were all the same. He chewed on grasses and continued to scratch himself. The Sun did not shine on him.

Across the fecund ground It slithered from the shade into the light and coiled at her feet. It was in love with her. Its eyes moved slowly over her. Nothing It had ever seen rivaled her flawless beauty. It listened to the slow exchange of her breath, in and out, in and out, the exchange in perfect harmony with the tree.

She saw It coiled at her feet in the soft grasses. She smelled the fragrance of the blossoms, felt the warmth of the sun on her skin, and heard the ripple of the joining rivers nearby. To her, the grasses, the blossoms, the sun, It, and the rivers were all the same.

It knew love, and because that love was unrequited, It knew pain.

Him and Her knew no love, they knew no pain, to them everything is everything. Except one thing, and this one thing they knew to be different and forbidden. How they knew this they did not know. They just knew. And because of that singular knowledge they avoided that which they knew to be forbidden... *for a while.*

It lay coiled at her feet, admiring her, staring at her, waiting. Waiting to be noticed. It watched her bathe and sleep. Across the entire garden it watched her gather food and eat. It noticed everything she did, and she noticed nothing about It.

It noticed she never, ever, ate the fruit from the tree.

Why do you not eat the fruit from the tree? It engaged her.

It is forbidden, she said.

It uncoiled and slithered right up to her perfect feet and pressed on, *Ahhh, is that so... And who forbade it?*

She stared at It and blinked.

Seizing the moment, It concluded, *It was I that forbade it.*

Again she blinked.

She reached down and picked up the ripened fruit at her feet. She took a bite. She became aware of the juice running down her chin. She noticed she was naked.

Who are you? It asked.

I am... She began but before she could finish It had returned to the hole from which It slithered, victorious.

At that very moment, far away in the Front Range of the high plains desert, a mother gave birth.

CHAPTER ONE

The Frailest Rabbit

On the hottest day of the year Hat Rabbit gave birth to three beautiful bunnies. One appeared stillborn. As was tradition, the mother nursed her newborns while the nurse-mother took the limp babe to the mouth of the old hole which overlooks the Front Range and laid him facing south, in a nest of soft down to await his return into the earth.

When rabbits die inside the warren, which is rare, most succumb to predators and are taken into the forest. The departed rabbits are placed at the mouth of the old hole to begin their return journey into the earth. According to rabbit beliefs, all rabbits must pass through the bowels of a predator in order to be reborn. By talon, claw, or jaw the lifeless rabbits are then carried away into the forest by bird, dog, or cat to be eaten, digested, excreted, and thus returned to the earth from which all life begins and ends. Again and again and again.

On the night Hat Rabbit birthed three beautiful bunnies and one apparent stillborn, the rabbits of her trace abandoned their warren near the old hole in pursuit of water. Hat Rabbit snuggled her babies in close, and together they began their trek. The animals that prey on the rabbits left the area as well. They always followed the rabbits, for rabbits are food, and food is life.

The frailest baby rabbit lay alone, not stillborn, and while facing the Front Range, its tiny heart was beating with the faintest rhythm.

♦

From the eastern horizon of the Front Range the Sun began his long upward journey, muttering to himself about locomotion: *Pushing peas with weakened knees up the stairs, again and again and again...* At the apex of his ascent he noticed the abandoned rabbit, lying on a bed of down, at the mouth of the old hole. He blew him a nourishing kiss before beginning his slow decent into the jagged horizon of the western mountains, muttering to himself as he went: *Bouncing balls down narrow halls, again and again and again...*

When the Sun had disappeared, the sliver Moon began her graceful arc across the Front Range. As most of her attention was elsewhere, she barely noticed the frail rabbit at the mouth of the old hole. When she saw him shivering and barely alive, she hummed him a warming lullaby and continued on her way across the night sky.

Day after day, night after night, the Sun and the Moon would nourish the rabbit, whisper him stories, and sing him songs.

The Sun spoke of all the great wars and fleeting triumphs of Earth's inhabitants from the beginning of time. He told tales of the great Runners, Febro and Marzo, and their marches into certain death and ultimate victories. He told of the rise and fall of great civilizations. Sun retold eons of earth's history, not as threads of details but as great movements, like water flowing in a river.

The Moon sang of feasts and weaving. She sang about the herbs, roots, and berries that aid in the healing of the sick; the dyeing of fabrics; the facilitation of death; and the instigation of spirit-walking. She sang of planting corn and beans and squash. She sang of birth and of death. She sang of migration.

Beside the Front Range at the mouth of the old hole the motionless rabbit, whom the Moon named Joonie for the month in which he was born, listened and learned. Although his eyes had never opened, he saw the world as described by Mother Moon and Father Sun with great clarity. With the nourishment of the Sun and the love of the Moon, the frailest rabbit survived and grew.

♦

One morning, just as Father Sun was peaking his head above the eastern horizon, Joonie asked him, *Am I dreaming?*

Dreaming? replied Father Sun. *Yes, as much as anyone, but more than most.* He began to mutter to himself. *I chase my head right out of bed and all day, long... long... long... At the break of dawn I stretch and yawn and start up the chase again... and again... and again.*

What? Come on, Father, Joonie quipped, frustrated with Father Sun's usual odd answers. *Seriously, Father, will I dream forever? Or will I wake up?*

Wake up? repeated Father Sun absently as he paced slowly across the sky. The idea of Joonie waking and leaving the mouth of the old hole and entering the cruel world was hard for him to bear. The Sun loved Joonie as his own child, and he knew when Joonie awoke he would face enormous challenges. But Father Sun and Mother Moon could not keep Joonie safe forever. Even the best of times are dangerous for rabbits, and Joonie had been born in the worst of times. Father Sun was aware of the impending plague and oppression that was soon to endanger all things living on earth. Father Sun rose and set many times before he finally answered Joonie's question.

One day, Joonie, you will wake up.

When? asked Joonie, surprised at the clarity of the answer.

Mother Moon and I need to talk, replied Father Sun. Then he grew silent and continued his arc across the sky.

Joonie lay as still as the day he was born and every day hence, thinking about what Father Sun had said.

He and Mother Moon need to talk? Joonie had discovered the murkiness in Father Sun's answer. *When are they going to do that? They are never in the same place at the same time.*

♦

When Mother Moon rose far on the eastern horizon, she was as full as a bubble.

As soon as her soft light shined on Joonie he asked her, *Do you and Father Sun ever speak to each other?*

Mother Moon glowed a soft orange from the smoke sent up by a forest fire in the valley below. *Father Sun and I do speak on occasion*, she replied.

When? asked Joonie.

Only during an eclipse.

Oh. When is the next eclipse?

I will wax and wane six more times before the next eclipse, said Mother Moon as she cast a gorgeous light onto Joonie. *Why do you ask? Did Father Sun say he needs to speak with me?*

Yes, he did. About me waking up.

A dark billow of smoke crossed Mother Moon's face. She knew that one day Joonie would leave the mouth of the old hole. She also knew the magnitude of the approaching threat and the challenges Joonie would have to overcome in order to survive.

Mother Moon looked down at Joonie. His feet were large for his body, but his legs were long and strong. His brown and white fur was soft. His ears, like his feet, were gangly and disproportionate. Mother Moon hoped he would grow into those someday. Joonie had become strong and healthy from the nourishment he received from Father Sun and Mother Moon.

But that was not all. Through the telling of stories they taught him about the depths of emotion, the corruption that comes with power, and the benefits of giving. They taught him about the seasons, the stars, and the tides. He learned many things about many things, except *how to live.*

♦

Joonie lay in wait for the seasons to pass. The stories he heard from Father Sun grew in intensity, and the world he had once imagined took on a darker hue. Mother Moon began her songs the moment she crested the horizon, and they did not stop until she disappeared behind the far western mountains. Her songs were about running and hiding. She sang of survival.

When the eclipse finally came, Joonie was anxious. The world he had imagined entering no longer felt safe.

During the next eclipse, Father Sun and Mother Moon spoke briefly as they passed each other in the sky.

We have prepared Joonie as best we can, said Father Sun getting straight to the point. *It is time for him to awaken.*

I never knew I could love like this again, said Mother Moon. *He is a beautiful child. Why does he have to face such hard times?*

For every grand cycle there is born a Runner to thwart the approach of the Iam. Fate has chosen Joonie. To be honest I don't know why Fate chose a rabbit, or the Runner before that, but she and I see things differently.

Is that because Fate has chosen to keep us apart?

Moon, we cannot blame Fate alone for the choices we make.

The eclipse was ending, and Mother Moon and Father Sun began to slowly separate. As their connection once again slipped away, Mother Moon whispered, *I will love you forever.* To which Father Sun replied, *And I you.*

Moon drifted past. Sun's first rays of light found the earth again. A mixture of their light shined upon Joonie, who opened his eyes for the first time.

♦

The rays that shone on Joonie also fell further north. There, the light was cast on something else. Something round. Something that moved. Now warmed, the crowning dome of a giant head breeched the crust of the red earth in a spray of dirt and dust.

With great effort, the creature forced its way upward through the hard-packed soil, struggling to push its enormous head through the small, dry opening. After the head popped through, its spindly limbs and emaciated body followed.

The creature's skin was covered in a thick layer of mud and fine, red dust that dried and cracked as it crawled out of the hole.

The oddity struggled to sit cross-legged before the mud dried. With great effort, it balanced it enormous head on its puny shoulders before it became immobilized by the baked, earthy crust that covered it. The creature's eyes were wide open under the crust, two moist circles. The creature came to rest there next to the hole, unmoving, its head like a round chunk of sandstone worn down by wind and rain and balanced upon a frail pillar.

A nearby obstinacy of bison witnessed the strange birth with dull interest as they ambled and chewed their cud. In time, the ambling obstinacy surrounded the precarious formation but was unconcerned by its presence. A passing bull smelled the moisture and salt from the creature's damp eyeholes and licked at them before moving on. Wrens perched on the dome momentarily before flittering off.

From there, the obstinacy expanded from horizon to horizon. Hundreds and hundreds of thousands of bison, heads down, grazed on the prairie grasses contentedly. The bison passed by the odd statue with only the occasional bull or cow stopping to lick the salt from the creature's eyes. They hardly noticed the *tap-tap-tapping* that came from inside the swollen head. They were oblivious as the creature's skull cracked like a clay egg.

But when a swarm of savage beasts burst out of the skull, screaming and tearing into the nearby bison, the obstinacy spooked. And thus began the stampede—the stampede that would become a harbinger signaling the dark coming of the Iam.

CHAPTER TWO

The Lone Rabbit

When Joonie's eyes opened upon the world for the first time, he was blinded by the intense Sunlight. He reflexively retreated into the darkness of the old hole. The Sun burned an image of the tree that was in front of the hole into his eyes.

Well, thought Joonie, his eyes aching trying to catch his breath, *this is a fine introduction to the world.* Joonie's first emotion as an awakened being was… *offended.*

He studied the purple-and-yellow image of the tree burned onto the back of his eyelids and noticed the silhouette of a creature looming in the branches. Joonie inched back into the hole and began to slowly reopen his eyes. As they adjusted to the darkness, Joonie saw the creature had moved from the tree branch and was now at the hole's entrance. A large body with a giant beak, no arms, and short, skinny legs hopped toward him.

The creature's talons clicked against the floor as it approached. It swiveled its sleek head. The creature stopped in front of Joonie, craning its neck to look at him with dark, beady eyes. The creature blinked and snapped its awful beak.

"My goodness," the creature cackled, "we thought rabbits left this place seasons ago. We haven't seen your kind around here for a long time."

Joonie peered at the creature as his eyes continued to adjust. He could not see well, but he knew what it was. Father Sun and

Mother Moon had described all of Earth's inhabitants to him, including the ravens.

"What you doin' here, rabbit?" prodded the raven. "Takin' a nap? Ain't you got food to produce?" The raven smirked and hopped around Joonie, looking at him intensely. Joonie stood still.

Rabbit? Joonie was shocked .

He took his eyes off the bird long enough to look down at his own… *paws.* It had never occurred to Joonie what kind of creature he was. The Sun and the Moon had failed to mention it, but he would have never guessed a rabbit. *A rabbit? Really? Rabbits are just fur-covered food on four legs. Everything eats rabbits. A rabbit's whole existence is to keep other creatures fed.* Joonie realized the situation he was now in. *Including ravens.*

The Raven moved closer. Joonie stared hard at the bird.

"You okay, rabbit?" asked the raven. "You look a little confused." The bird inspected the inside of the hole. "Who else you got with you? Never seen a lone rabbit. You got babies back in there? Or even better, you got a pregnant bunny with you?"

"Just me," said Joonie, surprised at the deep tone of his own voice. "I was out on a hunting expedition."

The raven burst out laughing. He pulled from under his wing a small pad of paper and a pencil. "Oh, rabbit, I must write this down. The unkindness will want to hear this one. A hunting expedition? That is really too much. What were you hunting? Berries? The elusive blueberry perhaps?" The raven continued to crack up. "Oh, wait, the ferocious butterfly. Where's your net, rabbit?"

The raven saw the intense look on Joonie's face and began to calm down from his laughter.

"Rabbit, what were you *really* hunting for?" asked the raven seriously.

Joonie stood up and took a step forward. He was taller than either he or the raven imagined. He looked down upon the bird.

"Ravens," said Joonie. "I was hunting ravens."

That took the bird by surprise. Joonie grabbed fast advantage and pushed straight past the raven, bolting toward the hole's entrance. Joonie tried to pivot around and say something else clever to the raven before he departed, but he was moving much too fast and skidded right out of the mouth of the old hole and tumbled head-over-heel down the steep embankment of the mountainside.

♦

"*Loco* rabbit," scoffed the raven, who was still standing in the hole bewildered.

All ravens are members of flocks called unkindnesses, and this particular raven, who was named *Mal,* was a member of the un-

kindness called El Garra. It was led by a brilliant raven whom everyone called Goyo.

"Just like a rabbit. All they do is run and hide." Mal paused as he recalled the Rabbit traces swarming with young and pregnant bunnies, "Well, I guess that's not all they do." Mal chuckled as he began to search the hole for the other rabbits he was sure were there. He bobbed up and down throughout the entire hole, but he didn't see any sign of the rabbits that must have been with Joonie.

Hmm, thought the raven as he exhausted all the nooks and crannies of the hole. *A lone rabbit. Never even heard of that. Maybe what the coyotes say is true. The world is going all topsy-turvy.*

Mal returned to the mouth of the old hole and looked down the steep hill that Joonie had just tumbled down. He could see no sign of him. *Lone rabbits hunting ravens,* Mal thought. Then he laughed and spread his wings and launched himself into the blue sky. *The world has gone crazy. Goyo will want to know about this.*

As he flew away from the mouth of the hole, he let out mocking caw and headed west into the dark, wild mountains.

CHAPTER THREE

Small Migrating Birds

Joonie bounced over rocks and roots, finally coming to an abrupt stop when he slammed into the trunk of a wide cotton-wood tree. Without thought, Joonie immediately jumped up and scampered about, looking for a small, dark hole to crawl into.

His instincts had taken over. He raced about trying to cram his body into any crack or crevice he could find. When he finally found cover under the low-lying branches of a scrub oak, he shoved his body under the bush as far as possible.

His heart was racing. He was so panicked he couldn't hold a thought in his head. His breath was rapid and shallow. Joonie was a mess.

Mostly he was just taken aback by what he was experiencing. "What… is… happening… to… me?" Joonie said, struggling to catch his breath. His eyes darted from side to side, looking for an exit. His large ears were deafened by the sound of his hammering heartbeat. His mouth felt as though he were chewing on dusty moth wings. Try as he might, Joonie could not gain control of his body. Then he remembered something that he heard in a story from Father Sun.

Humara the Runner, Father Sun had said, *could run for days without stopping, eating only a paste made from small seeds and the juice from the ground root of the cactus plant. He would deliver messages from Arana the Weaver, who lived near the source of all water, and her forbidden lover Bajo, who lived deep in Cobre Canyon, many, many miles away. His secret to running those great distances? He pulled his breath up through the soles of his feet...*

With this story in mind, Joonie wiggled his paws into the soft dirt beneath the scrub oak and focused on drawing his breath up through his body from "the soles of his feet." His shallow, rapid breaths began to expand. Eventually his breath became calm and controlled. It filled his body, and he slowly released it.

As he gained control of his breath, his mind followed. Joonie became still again, hidden under a bush at the bottom of the valley, alone in a world he had only heard about through stories.

♦

Mal the raven did not fly directly back to the tree of the unkindness to speak with Goyo. Instead he camouflaged himself in the high branches of a blue spruce over the den of the coyote band. Mal hoped to pick up some more information on the world going all topsy-turvy. The coyotes seem to know about events before they happened.

It was the heat of the day, so the pack was sprawled about sleeping in the shade of the blue spruce. Mal was not too late. Coyote bands, he knew, dreamt together. Each coyote dreams a part of a connected dream, and when they awake, each coyote shares his part of the dream. Together they understand the dream as a whole. All Mal had to do was hide until they awoke and listen to them put their dream together.

Settled onto the highest branch, Mal ruffled his feathers and waited.

One coyote began to stir. Another yawned a contagious yawn that infected the others. They were beginning to wake. Mal silently stretched his wings, retrieved his pad and pencil, and leaned forward to make sure he didn't miss a word.

Just then a small chickadee landed on the same branch upon which Mal was perched. "Hiya, birdie," said the chickadee in his singsong way.

"Raven," corrected Mal. "Now hush up."

"But *birdie*, yes? We are birdies?" continued the chickadee.

"And we have nothing in common," hissed Mal, "Now leave." Mal shooed away the chickadee with his big, black wing.

The tiny bird danced away a few inches and showed Mal his wing. "See this wing? See? Birdies have wings. *We are birdies.*"

Mal had little tolerance for such nonsense. He snapped his terrible beak at the small bird, which became startled and flew one branch above Mal. "Now be quiet," whispered Mal.

The little bird snapped his less than terrible beak and peeped very quietly, "See this beak, see? *We are birdies. We are, we are, we are.*"

Satisfied that the little bird had gotten the message, Mal turned his attention back to the coyote. When he looked down, all the coyote were awake standing in a tight circle, looking straight up the tree. Directly at Mal.

"Hello, birdie," mocked one of the coyote, which sent the others into hysterics. Mal watched as they loped away, noses to the forest floor, laughing as they went.

Mal looked up at the chickadee, which was now distracted by a gnat buzzing around his head. "Stupid bird," said Mal. "The ravens were about to get some information."

"Information?" asked the chickadee, not knowing what the word meant.

"You know, *news*. About the world going all topsy-turvy."

"Oh, news!" exclaimed the little bird. "Birdie has news, exciting news." The chickadee waited to be prompted, but all he got was an angry glare from Mal. "They are coming!" shouted the little bird.

"Who are coming?" asked Mal.

"Don't know who, don't even know what, just... They are coming! They are hungry!"

"How do you know this?"

"Migration," said the chickadee smugly, as if that explained everything. Which it did, actually. Mal knew that the little birds were the first to fly south or north each season, and they loved to bring news from the regions they'd left. The problem is, they always got their news wrong. "They popped up from the ground," the chickadee continued, "and gave the bison quiet a scare. The bison are running south now, crushing everything in their path."

“Bye, birdie.” said the chickadee suddenly. The little bird flew from the branch, leaving Mal all alone.

♦

Small, migrating birds—and the news they spread—have set a lot of ridiculous events into motion. One year, the little birds spread the news that Grandfather Tortoise, the oldest and wisest of all the animals, had died. The animals were devastated by the news and began to prepare for his return party. Thousands of animals had already begun the trek south to the far rim of Cobre Canyon, where Grandfather Tortoise lived, before it was revealed that he had been merely taking a deep siesta when the small birds had flown by.

The birds knew of the bison stampede, but only a few of the smallest and least reliable had witnessed what actually started it. What they didn't know is the first wave of Iam that hatched from the head of the earth-born creature were the Gira. The Gira had long, sinewy arms and round, muscular shoulders that were attached with no necks to shriveled heads with blackened eyes.

Their hands were razor-sharp claws, and draped between their wrists and their ridge-like spines were thin membranes of skin that looked like wings.

After the creatures had sprung from their sire's head, they hit the ground spinning, their wings billowing, their claws out, tearing into the flesh of the surrounding bison. The docile creatures were stupefied as they watched the whirling monsters slice into the herd. Bison dropped where they stood as the creatures tore deeper into the obstinacy.

The herd was so tightly packed they could not flee immediately. The bison closest to the murderous Gira began to push away from the slaughter, which in turn pushed the other bison. Like the creation of a tidal wave, it started as a faraway ripple and gained intensity the farther it traveled. This panicked flight from the Iam was the first ripple that would begin the Great Harbinger Stampede.

The small, migrating birds, with their flighty details, flew south singing, "*They are coming! They are hungry!*" From oak to pine to aspen, all across the Front Range, the little birds shared the exciting news. Had the birds been more reliable reporters, they would have flown down the valley warning the other animals, "*They are coming! Run for your lives!*" But they are small birds after all. They are, they are, they are.

CHAPTER FOUR

The Chased and the Prey

As the day wore on, Joonie stayed under the tight branches of the scrub oak trying to muster the courage to leave the security it provided. He was too scared to even peak his head from under the branches to look at the world around him. His own fear mortified him even more. Every time he moved, his heart raced and his breathing began to quicken again.

As Joonie sat still in the shade he noticed other feelings he had never experienced. He was thirsty. His tongue and throat were dry, and he had a crushing headache. His hollow stomach grumbled for attention. And finally he felt a random urge that bordered on uncontrollable: to find other rabbits. Particularly girl rabbits.

I have to move, Joonie thought. *If I don't, I will die here under a bush. That would really not be good.*

Joonie tried to remember stories that he had heard from Mother Moon and Father Sun, tales that might help him gather the courage to leave the overhanging bush. But he could only think of the stories Mother Moon had told before he awoke, stories of predators and of the importance of hiding which kept him rooted in place with fear. Joonie recalled hearing those stories and having empathy for the chased and the prey. But he never imagined that he would *be* the chased and the prey.

Joonie settled into his hidden nook and again took a deep breath. He began to dig his heels into the soft earth beneath him, exposing layers of decomposing leaves. He peered into the thatch of branches that covered him. At first it was like a thick blanket in which he could see nothing but patches of light. As he looked harder, though, he began to identify the layers of branches and the wide, open sky beyond. He could see clouds, distant mountains, and a tall dead cottonwood tree.

As Joonie focused on the tree, something high in the branches glinted. It was the golden eye of a hawk. The hawk blinked and slowly turned his head away from Joonie. He followed the hawk's stare and saw, through the branches, the perked-up ears of a coyote.

Joonie was being hunted. He knew that coyote found prey by watching hawks and stealing their prey from them. This coyote didn't seem to know where Joonie was, but he knew it was only a matter of time before someone would make a move.

"Hiya, bunny," chirped a small bird from out of nowhere. "Guess what?"

Joonie looked up. A little finch perched on a branch above his head. Several other finches were flitting about in the branches, chirping about clouds, pebbles, and dust motes.

"There's a coyote and a hawk hunting you. Did you know the bison are stampeding and some animals are gathering at the Confluence? Are you *alone*? Never seen a lone bunny before. Bye, bunny." The little finch flitted off.

Joonie's eyes returned to where the hawk was. Only now the hawk was gone. Joonie looked for the coyote, but it was gone as well.

His heart began to race. All Joonie could hear was the rush of his blood through his veins and the noise of the wind in the surrounding trees. As he extended his hearing, just like he had his vision, Joonie was able to pick up more distinct sounds. He heard feathers ruffle. The hawk had moved farther up the tree. The coyote stalked nearby, but the creature remained unseen.

Joonie continued to strain his ears, trying to pick up every sound he could. In the near distance he heard singing.

♦

Set 'em up, knock 'em down

Who's the baddest kid in town?

Roll 'em up, now move along

Before they get here you'll be gone.

Frozen with fear, Joonie tried to see where the song was coming from. He peered through the branches but couldn't see past a big, moss-covered rock.

The singing grew closer:

Grab your stuff and your new sweetheart.

We have no choice but to play our part.

The singer was on the other side of the moss-covered rock. Joonie was still. He waited.

The song stopped. All Joonie could hear was the gentle rushing of the wind.

Then he heard a new sound. Sniffing.

"You in there, rabbit?" asked a voice. "I can't smell you."

The sniffing sound was coming around the rock. The first thing Joonie saw was a stout nose twitching, trying to pick up the scent of the rabbit. Then he saw two small, wide-set eyes surrounded by a terrible headdress of spines.

Joonie recognized the creature from the teachings of Father Sun and Mother Moon. It was a porcupine.

The porcupine saw Joonie huddled under the bush and lay down with his head underneath the first few branches, his menacing hind-end facing outward.

"Are you really alone, rabbit?" he asked over his shoulder.

Joonie was too distraught to speak. He was still listening intently for any sound of the coyote and the hawk.

The porcupine seemed to sense Joonie's apprehension. He laughed. "Settle down, rabbit. The only way to get to you is through me, and I don't think that's going to happen. *Who's the baddest kid in town?*" He broke into song again for no apparent reason then continued speaking. "A little finch was just carrying on about a lone rabbit hiding under the scrub oak. There haven't been rabbits in these parts for seasons. Anyway, who's ever heard of a lone rabbit?

What happened? Are you the only one who survived?"

Joonie couldn't process so many questions. His throat was too dry, and his head continued to pound.

"You look terrible, rabbit."

Joonie looked at himself and saw he was covered in dirt, grass, and leaves. His fur was matted with sap. A deep sadness swept over him. Tears welled up in his eyes.

"Come on, buddy. My name is Pencilthin. Nothing's going to hurt you." The porcupine turned and gently offered Joonie a long-fingered paw. "Let's get you washed off."

Joonie was shaking as he took the porcupine's paw and was coaxed from the darkness of the bush and into the light of day. It was his first day as an awakened creature.

♦

After Joonie crawled out from the under the bush, he stood up and stretched his aching legs.

Pencilthin looked at him with wide eyes. "You're a pretty big rabbit."

For the first time, Joonie became self-conscious. Here he was—a big, lone, dirty, blubbering rabbit at the bottom of a valley. He began to sob.

Pencilthin, still gently holding Joonie's paw, led him down a nearby path. Joonie smelled the moisture and heard the bubbling of water. The prospect of drinking something quickened his pace, and soon he dunked his head in a small stream and gulped mouthfuls of cool spring water.

While Joonie drank, Pencilthin poured water from his cupped paws onto Joonie's fur and softly scrubbed away the sap and dirt. This tender act of kindness, as well as the refreshing water, filled Joonie's heart with warmth.

♦

Pencilthin, Joonie quickly found out, was as confident as he was formidably prickly. Joonie felt safe in the presence. After drying off from his drink and his bath, he relaxed. He lay on his stomach and chewed the clover that grew by the side of the small stream. The clover's taste was bitter at first, but as Joonie chewed, it began to sweeten in his mouth. A bee buzzed from flower to flower in front of Joonie's nose. His tired eyes crossed as they followed the bee, and soon he dozed off.

He was so exhausted he didn't notice that the porcupine had left him alone and exposed in a clearing next to the stream. He had been so desperate for water and food, he'd completely forgotten about being hunted. He hadn't even scouted for hiding spots that he could dart into.

Joonie awoke with a start, his heart in his throat. He looked around for Pencilthin. A high-pitched screech sounded from the treetop as the hawk, seemingly from out of nowhere, swooped down upon Joonie. The coyote sprang from his hiding place just outside the clearing, focusing on the prey the hawk was targeting.

Then the coyote saw Joonie. *That porcupine set me up!* he thought with disgust. For the second time in one day, Joonie felt offended.

The hawk's talons were outstretched. Its wings reeled upward as it pulled it out of its dive. The coyote was still in full sprint, clearly intending to plow right into the rabbit and pick up his stunned meal.

Joonie surrendered to the impact. The hawk let out a frantic screech and tumbled in a ball of wings and talons bouncing right over Joonie. Pencilthin charged toward the coyote, pivoted on his front paws, and reared his dreadful spikes.

The coyote had been sprinting so fast, he was unable to stop in time. He collided face-first with the brutal back-end of Pencilthin.

In pain, the coyote tried to tug his face from the porcupine's quills. After a few desperate attempts, the whining beast freed himself, taking with him a few dozen quills stuck deep into his flesh. One quill lanced his eye, popping it like a blister. Several protruded from his tender nose.

The coyote backpedaled and tried to regain composure, but Pencilthin was on him in an instant. Pulling a long quill from his impervious body armor, he grabbed the startled dog by the ear and thrust the long spike deep into the coyote's nostril, past his mouth, and into its brain, leaving the large dog lifeless.

Its wing wounded from the tumble, the hawk flew awkwardly onto a low-branch of an oak tree. It glared intently at Pencilthin. The porcupine turned to face the bird. Rather than offering up his defensive quills, he exposed his vulnerable underbelly to the bird, which seized its good fortune and flew at Pencilthin with its dreadful talons outstretched.

The hawk's attack was effective. The porcupine was knocked backward into the ground with such force that his quills stuck fast into the earth. Pencilthin could not move, and his tender belly was exposed to the hawk's next attack.

Joonie had been too afraid to even run away. He saw the hawk readying its death strike. Pencilthin was thrashing about, trying to get his quills unstuck from the ground. The bird launched into the air and wheeled around to begin its killing dive.

At that moment Joonie was receiving conflicting impulses. One said, *Run and hide, Joonie, run and hide.* The other impulse pleaded, *You've got to help the porcupine.* Before Joonie could think any more, he ran at Pencilthin and jumped over him, grabbing his flailing arm and pulling him out harm's way. The hawk came in too fast and slammed into the ground, but it quickly regained its balance and began to scratch at Pencilthin's face.

Joonie launched himself at the hawk. He grabbed the bird's outstretched leg and yanked. Joonie heard the hollow bone of the hawk's leg snap, followed by an awful screech of pain.

Pencilthin jumped on the back of the hawk and drove a long quill deep between the bird's wings. The hawk made a final attempt to become airborne before it collapsed in a heap of feathers.

The dead bird's golden eye staring directly at them with a look of intense hatred. Joonie shivered.

Pencilthin swaggered around the carcasses of the coyote and the hawk, his chest heaving, as if daring the dead beasts to rise again. He thrust his paw into the air and let out a primordial scream that raised the fur on Joonie's neck. Pencilthin then knelt, closed his eyes, let out an enormous breath, and clapped his paws.

Joonie felt exhilarated. But he was also terrified by what had just taken place. His foot was involuntarily thumping. He wanted more than anything to shout like the porcupine and beat his chest. At that moment, Joonie felt as if he could conquer anything.

Whatever it was that coursed through his veins, Joonie liked it. A lot.

♦

Attracted by the short but fierce battle, the many different creatures that lived in the valley near the stream began to fill the clearing. A smattering of small, migrating birds flitted from branch to branch excitedly. A couple of ravens landed in the top branches of a nearby tree. Two small, thirteen-striped chipmunks crept next to Joonie.

"Whoa," exclaimed one of the young chipmunks. "Pencilthin *is* the baddest."

"So I see," said Joonie.

Pencilthin knew that soon other coyotes in the band would pick up the scent of death and come to investigate. But he continued to kneel, taking deep breaths, purging his body of the fury that he had used to defeat the predators.

A scrappy little chipmunk kicked and flipped himself in the air, attacking an invisible foe before he tripped on his tail and tumbled in the dirt.

The other chipmunk pointed at his friend and laughed. Then he asked Joonie, "Are you Red Earth Trace? I didn't know their outer circles had reached this far. Where are the other rabbits?"

Joonie didn't know about the Red Earth Trace, but he did know a little about rabbit traces and warrens. The trace was the entire collective of rabbits that surround the warren, which was where the nurse-mothers, pregnant bunnies, and small bunnies live.

"A trace." Joonie repeated the words to himself as he looked around at the forest animals. The idea of being part of something greater than himself struck him like a quill in his guts when he realized he was not. He was alone. As the other animals cheered and celebrated, Joonie withdrew to the bank of the stream and peered at his blurry reflection in the rolling water.

♦

Pencilthin finally got to his feet and walked toward Joonie. The young chipmunks froze in place as he passed.

"Fear no dog," he said to them, "It's when they pack up that you have to worry."

He pulled two small quills from his back and handed them to the chipmunks. The little ones received these gifts with awe and immediately began to duel each other with them.

"Careful! You could…" Pencilthin began. Then he stopped. "Oh, never mind. Just have fun." He wanted to tell the little ones that killing another animal was nothing to celebrate. It was a gruesome responsibility. But he knew the little chipmunks wouldn't grasp that. They were too elated by the fact that two creatures that often killed chipmunks had themselves been killed.

Pencilthin once again took Joonie by the paw. Joonie looked at the porcupine's long fingers and was amazed at what great kindness and great destruction this paw could inflict.

"Come on, friend," said Pencilthin. "Let's go get some tea and soup at the Mushroom Den. It's been a hard day."

"You have no idea," said Joonie.

"You'd be surprised at what I know."

Together Pencilthin and Joonie walked down the path toward an ever-expanding world and a greater unknown.

CHAPTER FIVE

Traces, Warrens, Dens

The Sun had set, and the Moon was just beginning to shine a silvery light that illuminated the streamside path that Joonie and Pencilthin walked.

Joonie listened to the babbling of the stream and heard the porcupine draw deep breaths. As they walked in silence down the path toward the Mushroom Den, the forest became denser and darker. The stream no longer had obvious banks but leaked out on the path, which forced Joonie and Pencilthin to jump from exposed root to rock. When they did find drier ground, it was soft mounds of moss that gave way under their paws and puffed back into shape after they moved on. Tangles of fireflies illuminated the path like frenzied lanterns. A hatch of caddis flies emerged from a still pond, and cutthroat trout began slurping them off the surface of the water.

"Pencilthin?" Joonie began. He wanted to launch into a litany of questions for his viciously hirsute friend, but the porcupine put a finger to his mouth and shushed Joonie.

"It has been my experience, Rabbit," Pencilthin explained, "that talking about serious issues on an empty stomach results in rushed opinions and hurt feelings."

"But..." Joonie resumed. Pencilthin stopped him.

"Rabbit, I have a few steadfast rules. One of them is not to have a serious conversation on an empty stomach. I don't intend to break that rule tonight, so please, trust me. We'll talk about everything after we have a nice, hot bowl of soup and a cup of tea."

The notion of hot food made Joonie acquiesce. Still, he asked Pencilthin delicately, "What's another of your steadfast rules?" To which Pencilthin replied, "Hug a porcupine at your own peril."

♦

After a while Joonie heard a deep rhythm coming from down the path, a rhythm like a slow heart beat. *Dwub dwub... Dwub dwub... Dwub dwub.* As they neared the sound, Joonie saw a tremendous fallen tree. It was hollow and filled with luminescent mushrooms. Forest creatures sat around drinking, eating, and talking. There was a sound of laughter and conversation. The *dwub dwub... dwub dwub...* came from the bloated throat of a bullfrog that was sitting with a group of amphibians, smoking water pipes and playing a board game. Offsetting the frog's bass pulse was the repetitive hammering from a lofted woodpecker: *Dwub dwub tit tit, dwub dwub tap. Dwub dwub tit tit, Dwub dwup tap.*

Joonie honed in on the added harmonics of the cricket's fiddle and the crescendo of the winds that murmured through the leaves. *Now this is more what I had in mind for my waking life,* he thought as he took in the scene of beautiful light, pleasant sounds, and happy animals.

The mushrooms that surrounded the fallen tree glowed radiant greens and soft blues. Some were rimmed with white and gradually yellowed toward the center. A brilliant cluster of toadstools near the rotting mouth of the tree glowed red and orange like a bonfire and was surrounded by a number of squirrels engaged in their squirrelly histrionics.

Giant puffballs had been carved into tables crowded with river otters, marmots, squirrels, and beavers drinking fermented mushroom tea from carved wooden mugs and eating platters filled with wilted purslane, rosehips, roasted morels, and pinenuts. Many of them were engaged in games involving shells, dice, or cards. A gang of white-tailed deer bucks tussled for the attention of a doe

that was busy serving drinks and picking up dirty mugs from empty tables. Behind the clashing bucks, a marmot took bets from a rafter of turkeys on the outcome of the ridiculous display of bravado.

Pencilthin led Joonie through the menagerie toward two porcupines that were locked in a staring contest. When they became aware of Pencilthin approaching, they reluctantly broke off their contest and called a timeout. One of the porcupines grabbed a passing pika who was serving drinks to the other forest creatures.

"Hey, get this guy a cuppa tea," the porcupine said, gesturing at Pencilthin with his lifted mug. "If what the little birds say is true, he just took out a band of bloodthirsty coyotes."

"Well," said Pencilthin, pulling himself onto a large, flat-topped mushroom, "it's not like the little birds to misinform." He laughed and stretched out belly-down on the cap.

Joonie had not approached the table. He stood a little way off, fighting a sudden urge to run and hide. Now that he was growing accustomed to this new place, he found he was overwhelmed and still a bit offended that Pencilthin had used him as bait to attract the hawk and the coyote. He was tired, hungry, and ashamed.

Ashamed of *what*, he had no idea. He just knew he was. All he wanted to do was cry and sleep.

"C'mere, rabbit, and get some tea and soup in you," said Pencilthin. "It will do you more good than you can possibly imagine."

The two other porcupines scooted over to make room for Joonie. This simple gesture of inclusion from Pencilthin and his brethren warmed Joonie's heart, and he abandoned his instinctive fear and joined the small prickle of porcupines.

♦

The pika returned to the table with two cups of fermented mushroom tea and a pot of soup made from wild burdock, dandelion greens, and dried stigmas from the purple-spring crocus, the latter of which gave the soup a beautiful lavender color. Another pika came by with a basket of freshly baked, sprouted-grain rolls.

Joonie and Pencilthin abandoned their social obligations and became entirely absorbed by the wonderful meal in front of them. The two porcupines took advantage of their occupation with the food and returned to their staring contest.

Joonie was so hungry that he didn't realize the food he was consuming was unbelievably delicious until he'd eaten half a bowl of soup and downed three rolls. As he slowed his chewing, he experienced flavor combinations for the very first time. The tastes melted and swirled on all sides of Joonie's tongue. The flavors were like the warmth he felt when he received kind gestures from Pencilthin. He chewed the thin slices of burdock and dipped his rolls into the piquant broth. Everything in the soup combined perfectly. More than just a sum of its parts, the soup was an entity unto itself.

Joonie had gulped down half his mug of tea before he became aware of all the intricate flavors of smoke, spice, and wood it had to offer. He kept the tea in his mouth, swishing it around, savoring its nuances.

The pika returned to the table. "Oh, what didn't you like about the soup?" he asked Joonie with a wink, looking down into the rabbit's almost empty bowl.

"Incredible," was all Joonie could say.

"Drink your food and chew your tea, that's the key," sang the Pika as he picked up the empty basket of rolls. "More?"

"Yes, please," said Joonie, "and more tea, if you have any."

"Oh, we've got plenty of tea," said the Pika as he walked toward the wide mouth of the fallen tree which housed the kitchen. "Mind its effects, however. It hits everyone differently." The dueling porcupines simultaneously nodded in agreement, never breaking eye contact.

Joonie wasn't sure if it was the effect of the tea or the nourishing meal, but he felt magnificent. He wasn't even tired anymore. Digging his paws into the soft earth, he leaned back into a puffball that had been carved into a reclining chair and stretched his arms behind his head. He let out a very satiated sigh.

"You look much better, rabbit," said Pencilthin, joining him in a position of tranquil repose. "Before we ate, you looked like you were about to burst into tears."

Joonie grinned, and a laugh flew out of his belly like a pandemonium of hummingbirds. Once it got going, he couldn't stop. His cheeks ached and his eyes watered as he tried to regain composure, but the laughter kept rolling out.

The tea may indeed be having an effect on me, thought Joonie. And he laughed some more.

♦

"Pencilthin?" said Joonie after he'd finally stopped laughing. "My belly is full now, and I would really like to talk about what I saw today."

"Okay, Rabbit. Let's talk. What do you want to know? "

"Where did you learn to fight like that? "

"The way to overcome a predator," Pencilthin answered cryptically, "is to betray your instincts." He reminded Joonie of Father Sun and the vague answers he would give him.

Pencilthin saw the blank look on Joonie's face. "Predators and prey are both exasperatingly predictable. They behave in exactly the same way all the time. Predators know their prey's habits and hunt them successfully because of that knowledge. The prey needs to know the predator's tendencies and alter its own behavior to confound the hunter. By not behaving predictably the predators don't know what to do giving the prey a chance to escape."

Or attack. Thought Joonie.

Pencilthin scooted up to the edge of the puffball. "For example when provoked, porcupines will stop, tuck in their heads, and point their business ends at their attacker. We do this every time without fail. Squirrels always scamper up a tree, always, even if they are being chased by a bobcat who can also climb trees. When threatened, trout dart toward the deepest part of pool. And rabbits…"

"Run and hide," finished Joonie.

"Precisely."

"But you charged straight toward the coyote."

"He never saw it coming. And you snapped a hawk's leg. That's not very rabbit-like of you." Pencilthin laughed.

The two other porcupines broke eye contact and turned toward Joonie. "You did what?" they asked in unison.

♦

Before Joonie could answer, the two bucks tussling for the attention of the serving-doe locked antlers. Their heads entwined, they pulled and pushed through the Mushroom Den, frantically trying to get unstuck.

The patrons of the Den secured their mugs of tea and plates of food and cleared out, making room for the deer but staying near enough to enjoy the show. It didn't take long for the marmot to circulate amongst the forest creatures, taking bets on which deer would end up on its rear. There was shouting and laughter as the brawl intensified.

Just as the buck fight was reaching a pitch, a commotion issued from the kitchen just inside the mouth of the hollow tree. The forest creatures parted, and a grumbling was heard from inside.

"This nonsense had better be over by the time I get out there," warned a female's voice punctuated by the clanking of pots and pans.

The bucks continued to push and pull at each other as the owner of the voice stalked out of the kitchen carrying a large wooden spoon.

To Joonie's surprise, it was a rabbit. She wore an apron, and her ears were tied back with a scarf. She was followed out of the kitchen by seven little bunnies bounding about her feet. She walked up to one of the bucks as it prepared to rear back on his hind legs and grabbed him by the nose. Then she twisted with her left paw, and with her right she popped the other buck upside the ear, causing him to twist in the opposite direction.

As if by magic, the bucks' antlers unlocked. She still had not released the one buck's nose, though, and continued to twist it until his eyes began to water.

"Ow, stop it, please," the buck pleaded.

"No," said the rabbit, twisting harder.

"Please, please stop," whined the buck.

Finally the rabbit pushed the buck onto his tail. A small cheer erupted from the animals that won the bet. The abashed buck slunk off into the forest. The rabbit marched toward the other deer, who stopped rubbing his sore ear and took off in a flash as he saw the rabbit approaching.

The fight abruptly over, the forest animals returned to their food and games. The rabbit straightened her apron and turned toward the kitchen when she noticed Joonie sitting next to Pencilthin on the puffball.

"Aren't you Red Earth Trace?" she asked him directly. "Where are the others?"

Joonie was captivated by this rabbit. Pencilthin poked Joonie in the ribs with his elbow. "N-no, I am not Red Earth Trace,"

Joonie stammered. “I am Joonie.”

“Part of the Joonie Trace?” asked the rabbit. “Never heard of it,”

“No, I’m just Joonie,”

The rabbit dropped her spoon onto the forest floor. “You have a *name*?”

Pencilthin looked at Joonie. His eyes grew wide.

One of the little bunnies picked up the dropped spoon and ran after her siblings, who were bumping and rolling at their mother’s paws. The rabbit called over to one of the pika, “Have beaver cook off the rest of those morels, and bring me a mug of tea.” She took off her apron and sat down with Jonnie and Pencilthin.

“Who gave you the name Joonie?” she asked.

“Well, my mother did.”

“And what Trace is your mother from?”

Joonie did not want to jump right in and say he was raised by the Sun and Moon while he lay dreaming at the mouth of the old hole. Sitting here on the mushroom cap, that life no longer felt real. Joonie could not even be sure that it ever was.

“The name Joonie was not given to you by a rabbit,” the cook said with absolute certainty.

"How do you know that?"

"Because rabbits don't have names. Only the Trace has a name. There is no such thing as an individual rabbit. Each rabbit is merely a small part of the bigger organism known as the Trace."

Joonie mulled over this concept. "Like soup," interjected Joonie.

"What?" said Pencilthin.

"The soup we just ate was more than just the individual ingredients that were put into it. It was something more. It was *soup*."

"Soup?" The rabbit thought about this. "Mmm, maybe, yes. A soup is something more than its ingredients. I like that, Joonie."

Joonie flushed with warmth at the compliment. Then Cook Rabbit began telling Joonie all about rabbits, traces, and warrens. What he came to understand is that traces are made up of concentric circles that extend outward from the warren. The outer circles are made up of the feeders, those rabbits that are not mature enough to start reproducing or too old to reproduce anymore. The middle circles are made up of the breeders. The core of the trace is the warren, where the nurse mothers, pregnant and birthing rabbits, and small bunnies live. As long as the predators prey on the feeders and leave the breeders and the warren alone, the trace will continue to thrive and the predators will remain fed. There is no sense of loss among the trace when individual rabbits are eaten as long as the trace survives.

"What trace are you?" asked Joonie.

"Bedbug Trace, the smallest Trace in known history," Cook Rabbit said. Then she laughed, looking down at the seven bunnies bounding about the puffballs. "And the Mushroom Den is our warren. I feel as if all the animals that come to the Mushroom Den are part of our trace. I was once part of the Points West Trace but got carried away when the river swelled in a big rain. After washing up on the shore near here I carried myself to the Mushroom Den, drenched and weak. The animals took me in and nursed me back to health."

"You were a lone rabbit like me," said Joonie, his voice full of affection.

"Yes. And it was the strangest feeling. It was like I had lost the use of my senses. I tell you, Joonie, since I was amputated from my trace I have never felt whole again. Rabbits aren't supposed to feel alone. But I do." She dabbed at the corner of her eye with her apron. "I don't know if I'll ever feel whole again."

♦

Joonie looked at Cook Rabbit tenderly, and she looked at him. At that moment he felt an overwhelming need to become part of the Bedbug Trace.

A flock of small, migrating birds descended onto the branches of the oak trees that surrounded the Mushroom Den. The birds were making a frantic dissonance.

"The coyotes are coming! The coyotes are coming! The coyotes are coming!"

Pencilthin grabbed Joonie. "Now is the time to run and hide," he said. "Meet me at the Confluence in three days. Now go!"

Joonie turned to find Bedbug and her trace, but they had already fled.

Joonie bolted down the path in what he hoped was the opposite direction from the approaching coyote. Again he was alone.

CHAPTER SIX

Ghost Cat

Joonie bounded down the path, clumsily ducking into one hiding spot, thinking better of it, and scampering to another just to panic and bolt off again.

Within seconds of the little birds' alarm, the entire Mushroom Den had been evacuated, leaving no signs that a supper party had just been in full swing. The plates, bowls, mugs, and board games that had been in use moments before miraculously disappeared along with the patrons.

The music of the forest was gone. Only the increasing wail of the wind through the trees remained. Joonie heard the baying of coyotes in the distance. As he jumped out of his latest hiding spot, he smacked his head hard on the edge of a rock. He began to bleed.

"Joonie," he heard Bedbug whisper. "Over here, quickly."

Joonie saw Bedbug Trace peering out of a hollow knot in the base of a cottonwood tree.

"Hurry," the trace called.

In two leaps Joonie reached the security of the hollow. "Oh, dear," said Bedbug. "You're bleeding." She began to lick the blood from Joonie's forehead.

"I'm okay," said Joonie, blushing.

"Shhh," whispered Bedbug. The padding of the coyote paws could be heard outside the hollow. "They must have smelled the blood."

Joonie recognized immediately the danger he had put the trace in and began to bolt out of the tree. Bedbug grabbed him as the shadow of a coyote crossed in front of the hollow. The coyote let out a howl of excitement that sent the rabbits scrambling to the far wall of the hollow knot.

Joonie trembled with fear. The Bedbug Trace huddled near him, as far from the entrance as possible. He was shaking so badly he could barely stand. Bedbug put a paw on Joonie to try to calm him. All was quiet.

In an instant, the head of a coyote filled the entrance of the hollow knot. The beast growled and spit on the rabbits, but they were just out of reach of his bared teeth. His yellow eyes were trained on Joonie.

Joonie began to feel woozy as the terrifying scene came in and out of focus. The sound of more paws came from outside. The whole coyote band hurled itself at the tail-end of the coyote whose head was stuck in the hollow, pushing his fearsome head deeper into the tree.

The coyote grabbed one of Bedbug's bunnies in his awful jaws and pulled him out of the opening. In a flash, a smaller coyote pushed his head into the hollow and snatched two more bunnies. Bedbug tried to shield her young, but it was no use. Joonie remained frozen in the far corner, just out of reach. Before he passed out he saw Bedbug herself violently pulled out of the hole.

Then everything went dark.

♦

Linens and lions, clothes a dryin', all depend on me… on me… on me…

Joonie heard the familiar words of Father Sun's ascension mantra.

Am I dreaming, Father? asked Joonie.

Yes, came Father Sun's familiar voice. *As much as anyone, but more than most. Leaves a turnin', forests burnin', all because of me... of me… of me…*

Father, pleaded Joonie, *what do I do?*

The Sun continued on his path, chanting.

Please, Father, said Joonie. *Help me, I am so afraid.*

Give the fear a name, said Father Sun as Joonie began to awaken.

Joonie opened his eyes. The Sun was out, and the forest seemed to have forgotten the massacre of the night before. The creek babbled. The birds chirped. Dew clung to the plants.

But Joonie had not forgotten. He was devastated. And angry. With the words of Pencilthin in his head—*The way to overcome a predator is to betray your instincts*—Joonie got to his feet with a newfound intensity and focus.

My instinct is fear, thought Joonie. *In my short life I've been crippled by it. And now because of my fear the smallest rabbit trace is gone. I will not hide, but I will run all the way to the Confluence.*

Joonie left the hollow knot and looked down the path in both directions. He knew if he followed the watercourse it would eventually lead to the Confluence where he was to meet up with Pencilthin.

Joonie took a few apprehensive hops down the path and stopped. *Something is watching me,* he thought, sniffing the air.

No, that is your fear, came a conflicting inner voice. *There is nothing watching you.*

Joonie hopped down the path a few feet more, feeling the unseen watcher getting closer. He could sense the eyes on him. His fur tingled. His heart raced. Whatever it was, it was getting closer.

Joonie felt something right behind him. He spun around. There was nothing.

It's just my imagination, he assured himself. The forest was quiet. Only the chirping of a few birds and the hammering of a woodpecker could be heard. Joonie was only four feet from the hollow he'd just left.

At this pace, I'll never make it to the Confluence in three days.

Downstream on the bank, a large boulder created an eddy that swirled with sticks and foam. *I will run to that boulder,* thought Joonie. *Go!*

Joonie bolted as fast as he could to the boulder, feeling as if the unseen watcher were nipping at his heels. The sensation of being chased was so real that when Joonie got to the boulder, he buried himself in a small hole under the big rock.

After the sprint, Joonie was completely out of breath. *No, this*

will never do! I will not hide. I will not hide. Joonie crawled out from under the rock and back onto the path. Then still catching his breath, he picked out another landmark in the distance and ran to it.

This time he did not run at full speed. Instead he stretched himself out, which allowed him to cover more distance with less effort. He was less winded when he arrived, but he could not shake the feeling of being hunted. The anxiety soured like a sickness is his stomach.

Joonie picked out yet another landmark, a boulder far downstream and ran toward it. His front paws stretched way out in front of him. His strong hind legs propelled him. He felt his spine elongate, which allowed his ribs to separate slightly. His lungs had more room to breathe. Holding his head high and pushing his chest out, Joonie adjusted to his up-and-down locomotion. The forest blurred by him on either side. Focused on his running form, he forgot about his unseen predator.

I'm running! He felt ecstatic. Yet as Joonie neared the boulder, his fear returned in force and he stumbled. He was sure he felt the hot breath of the predator on his back. Too scared to turn around, he regained his footing and ran in a panic to the boulder. He lay there panting. Waiting. *I can't do this. My fear is too great. It is a part of me. I can't overcome it.*

"Just come and get me already!" Joonie screamed into the forest. "I quit. I don't want to live. Just come and finish me off!" He rolled onto his back, surrendering to whatever may come.

"No," said a pouty voice. It seemed to come from inside Joonie's head and from the forest at the same time. "I'd rather toy with you. It's fun for me."

Joonie flipped onto his belly and crouched lightly on his paws.

"Who said that?"

"Me," said the voice.

"What?"

Joonie scanned the forest for the source of the voice. For a moment he thought he saw green eyes shining from under an overhanging rock, but when Joonie blinked, the eyes were gone. A cluster of leaves danced in the wind along the path.

"Just get it over with," he said. "I can't run and hide anymore. I'm just a dumb bunny. I'm scared of my own shadow. I'm all alone, and I killed the smallest rabbit trace."

"You killed an entire rabbit trace?" said the voice. "That is impressive. Maybe you're not so weak after all."

"I didn't kill them myself. The coyotes did. I got them killed because I'm a dumb, scared bunny, and I ran into their hiding place with blood on my head."

"Hmm," the voice purred, "that is bad. A rabbit *is* an odd choice for a Runner."

"What?" said Joonie. His ears perked up at the word "Runner."

"Oh, not this again. I said you are an odd choice to be a Runner. Particularly in the light of the approaching Iam."

The green eyes seemed to glitter again in the shadows.

Of all the stories Father Sun had told him, the ones about the Runners were Joonie's favorites. Joonie loved the stories of Humara and the Thousand-Mile Horse Race and Mecurio's Journey into the Underworld. Runners were the bravest and strongest beings on earth. In ancient times the gods used the Runners to carry the most important messages.

One time Mecurio made a bet with Big Black, the mountain god, that he could run around the world. Big Black had the highest vantage point of all the gods and knew that the land bridge that linked the two continents had been destroyed. Mecurio would never be able to run the entire circumference of the world. But Mecurio knew this too and had trained himself to run on the ocean floor. When he arrived at the collapsed land bridge, he burdened himself with heavy weights and ran into the water. He ran across the ocean floor and surfaced on the other side.

Snapping out of his reverie, Joonie thought he saw a large, silver shape move nimbly under the overhang and disappear.

"Who are you?" Joonie asked again.

"As fate would have it, I am the one who will teach you to run. Or I will eat you." The voice laughed. "The choice is yours."

CHAPTER SEVEN

From the Hole

Zero, the fattest black-tailed prairie dog in the village, popped from her hole in the midst of the bison herd. She was still bleary-eyed from her long nap, one that was interrupted by an annoying tap-tap-tapping sound.

She blinked in the bright, midday Sun and focused on the odd-shaped rock that had somehow appeared outside her hole since the time she fell asleep. The tap-tap-tapping sound seemed to be coming from inside this precariously shaped formation. The bison and the other prairie dogs in her village seemed unconcerned as they grazed around it peacefully.

Zero was hungry from her sleep, so she joined the other dogs and began munching on the broad leaf weeds that grew next to the prairie grass that the bison were grazing on. Zero sniffed the air and detected a slight hint of moisture.

The tap-tap-tapping continued as the oblivious animals surrounded the odd rock. Zero felt a slight tremor and bolted toward her hole, but the other animals seemed unaware. She cautiously returned to her grazing, keeping a wary eye on the rock

"Did you feel something?" Zero asked a nearby prairie dog. The other dog just kept grazing, so she asked again, "Uh, did you notice the ground shake?" The other prairie dog continued to ignore her and sauntered off.

Zero felt another slight tremor. She looked toward the rock.

"Did you see that?" Zero yelled this time. "I swear that rock just moved." The other prairie dogs grazed unconcerned.

"What is that thing?" she asked a bison whose ear was near her. The bison blinked and blew hot breath forcefully from his nose. But he said nothing.

Zero rubbed her eyes and wondered if she were still asleep.

And then… *CRACK!*

Zero looked over at the round top of the rock and saw a giant split in it.

CRACK!

The rock split in half. Bursting from that shell came the whirling devils known as the Gira.

The bison lifted their heads and saw the Gira. With their razor-sharp claws and tireless muscles, they begin spinning toward the bison, ripping into their hides and tearing out chunks of flesh. The panicked bison fled the vicious attackers. In their haste they trampled the prairie dogs and crushed their village.

Zero was stuck under the fallen roof of her hole. She watched in terror as the Gira flung themselves into the unsuspecting bison, murdering them mercilessly and leaving the others wounded and dying on the ground. The bison nearest the Gira pushed hard against the others in the herd, which in turn pushed them into the bison ahead.

Within moments the peaceful prairie had turned into complete chaos.

Zero, immobile with fear and the weight of the roof, watched as a tall, stovepipe hat begin to emerge slowly from a hole near the crumbling shell. From the hole in the earth came the Alooshi, long, thin creatures that walked erect on two legs and were painted black with white hands and white circles around their eyes. On their heads they wore stovepipe hats, and around their necks were thick chains.

Zero closed her eyes as the angular creatures stalked with their long legs after the Gira. When she opened them again she saw an Aloosh take the chain from around his neck and begin swinging it overhead. Then he released it. It flew from his hand and wrapped itself around the legs of a whirling Gira. The Gira thrashed wildly as the Aloosh approached and picked it up, binding its terrible claws behind its back and forcing a tablet of some kind down the its throat. Within seconds the Gira collapsed on the ground as the Aloosh retrieved his chain and stalked after another Gira.

Zero whimpered as she looked out over the hundreds of dead and wounded bison and prairie dogs. Struggling to free herself from the collapsed hole, she soon began to tire. The Gira chased the bison, and the Alooshi chased the Gira. A great cloud of dust had been kicked up, and the Sun's light began to fade underneath it. The cries of distress from the wounded animals could barely be heard above the thundering noise of the stampede. The air filled with the scent of blood and panic.

A few Alooshi stayed behind and chipped away at the dry hole from which they came. Using long pick axes, they expanded its circumference. Sparks and chunks of earth flew from the impact of each strike. Zero held her breath as the next set of creatures began to emerge from the hole.

Squeezing through the expanded hole came the Tar-Reefs, corpulent bipeds with enormous eyes protected by thick goggles and stout upturned noses punctured by gaping nostrils. The Tar-Reefs carried with them black, wide-mouthed bags filled with tabulating, measuring, and other devices used in accounting.

Upon seeing a bison dead on the ground, the Tar-Reefs opened their bags and pulled out large, white sheets and spread them on the red earth. On the sheets they laid their sharp, metallic tools: knives, clamps, saws, drills. Two Alooshi spread the hind legs of the bison as the Tar-Reefs sliced into its belly and began carefully pulling out the entrails and vital organs, weighing them on a device and placing them neatly on the white sheet that was soon stained with blood.

Another Tar-Reef jotted down numbers with a stubby pencil in a book filled with rows and columns. Within moments the bison was reduced to its many parts, and the Tar-Reef moved on to tabulate something else, leaving the flesh to rot.

Zero grew woozy. The Tar-Reef, eyes and noses down, turned toward her direction, picking up and examining every stone and plant underfoot. She tried not to look as the fat tabulators picked up a dead prairie dog and reached into their bags for their gory instruments.

A Tar-Reef spotted Zero, stuck fast in the hole. He whistled

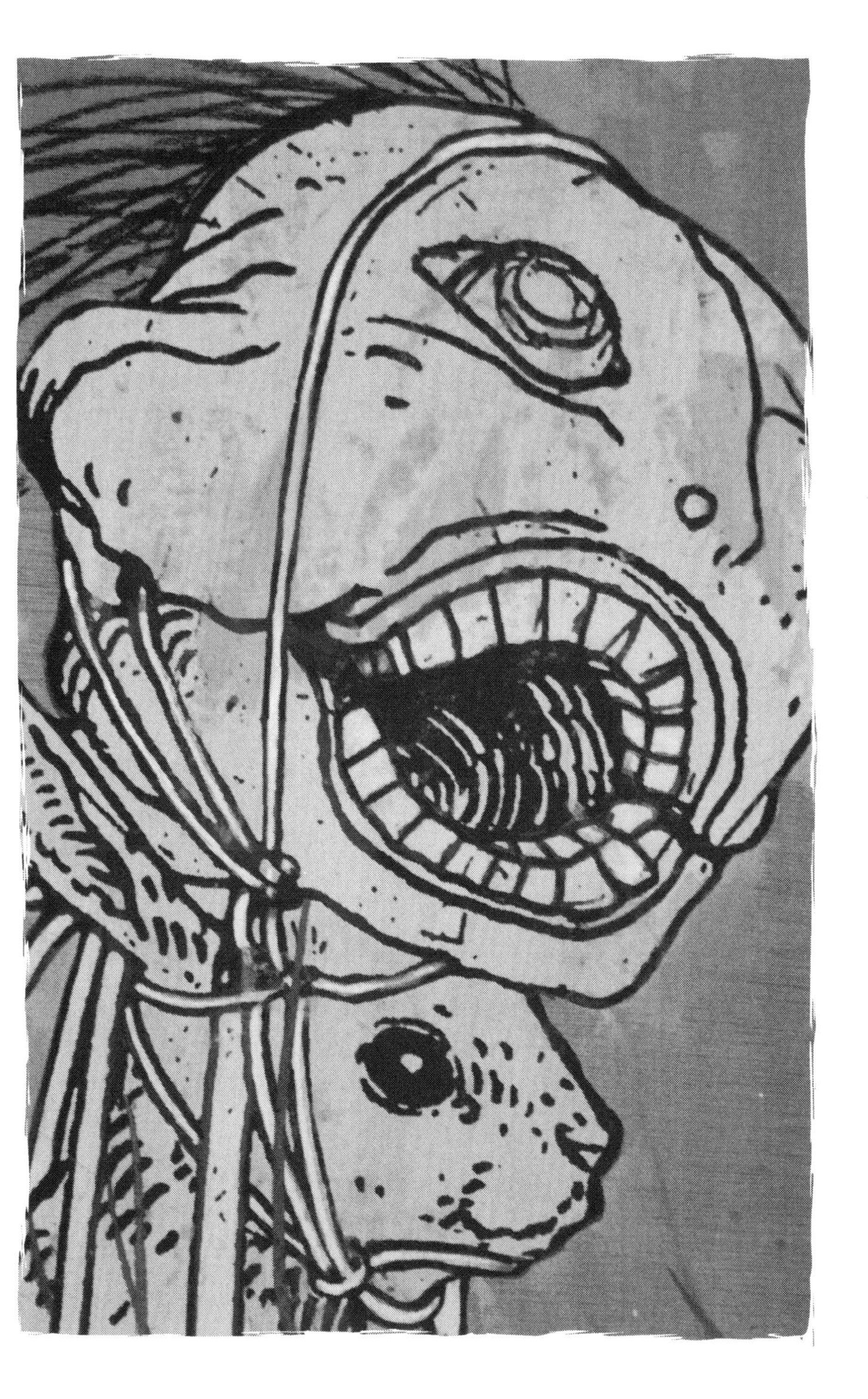

loudly through his nose, and another Tar-Reef began to walk toward her.

The creature reached for Zero. It wore thick gloves. Its eyes were magnified behind the goggles. She could see the red veins pulsing in the whites of its bulging eyes. She screamed and bit at the Tar-Reef as it forcibly pulled her from the hole.

But right when Zero couldn't take anymore, the beast dropped her and turned toward the hole.

A cloud of red dust erupted. Two more Alooshi emerged. These Alooshi were colored the opposite of their predecessors, with bodies painted white, hands black, and black rings around their eyes. On their heads they wore no hats, but their bald pates were painted crimson. They stood by the hole's edge, arms crossed, awaiting the next arrival.

Through the haze of dust and death, Zero saw another biped creature emerge from the blackness of some unseen underworld. This one was wrapped in a crimson robe. Covering its face was an expressionless white mask. Two piercing, blue eyes radiated from behind the mask. Perched on its shoulder was a tethered, red-tailed hawk. This androgynous figure was the Overseer, the orchestrator of the surface breech.

The Overseer scanned the shield of stampeding bison bolting south then looked up at the clouds of dust billowing into the sky. Then he walked to the blood-soaked sheet that contained the vivisected bison and examined at first the organs, then the hide that lay flat on a separate sheet. Moving on, he picked up the bison's brain and, after a quick examination, placed it on the hide.

"Find the Runner," the Overseer instructed his red-tailed hawk in a soft voice.

The hawk lifted itself into the air and began the search.

Following the Overseer came hundreds of monkeylike creatures led out of the hole by the Alooshi. These new beasts were covered in scales, and their enormous heads were made up mostly of mouth and teeth. In their hands they carried wooden clubs dotted with hard knots. They were known as the Wadi. Each time an Aloosh walked by with an unconscious Gira to throw back in the hole, the Wadi howled and pounded their clubs onto the earth, and their tiny black eyes glowed red.

Under the obscurity of the rising dust cloud, the Iam army was being assembled.

"Follow the bison," the Overseer ordered one of the white-on-black Alooshi.

"What of the Runner?" the Aloosh asked.

"Once again it's a funny game fate is playing," the Overseer said. "This time she chose a rabbit."

The Aloosh laughed, "A rabbit? That is funny."

The Overseer grabbed the Aloosh by its chain and pulled him down onto his knees. "Even the tiniest ripple can turn into a tidal wave. Never underestimate the power of small things." He turned away, shaking his head. "Or slow ones."

From her hole Zero looked up through the rising dust and saw the Moon following the Sun in what once was a blue, cloudless sky. Wounded and tired, she slowly crawled away from the mounting army. Her entire coterie of prairie dogs had been destroyed in the turmoil. Picking her way carefully through the forest of hooves and legs she began her journey west out of the valley, where she hoped to stay alive long enough to alert the animals of the Iam army.

CHAPTER EIGHT

Without Ceremony

Joonie was not sure if the silvery cat with green eyes, the one that moved like a ghost from underneath the overhang, was real or a dream.

His departure from the peaceful dream world into the harrowing adventure of waking life was so abrupt, his young mind was having difficulty distinguishing between the two. Joonie felt the fear rise up through his feet and gnarl in his stomach. Staring intently at Ghost Cat, Joonie connected to his breath and exhaled his fear. With purpose Joonie moved around the boulder, taking his eyes off Ghost Cat for a moment as he looked down stream.

"Aren't you going to run, rabbit?" asked Ghost Cat as she sat on her haunches and licked her massive paw.

"Joonie. My name is Joonie. And yes, I prefer that option to the other you offered, to be killed. I just want to get an idea of where I'm going to run."

As soon as the last word left Joonie's mouth, he saw Ghost Cat's whiskers twitch. The cat sprang toward him. But Joonie bolted and was well past the boulder by the time the cat was into her second stride.

The path was wide open with a lattice of exposed roots and dotted with river rock, which Joonie gracefully bounded over. Ignoring his instinct to hide, Joonie ran right down the middle of the path. The cat was fast and on Joonie's heels in seconds.

"This is too easy," Ghost Cat said, rearing back her paw to swipe Joonie's hind legs. Joonie saw the cat's paw, claws retracted, hovering behind him, ready to strike. When Ghost Cat swiped, Joonie jumped over the oncoming paw. Then he circled behind the cat and, with all his might, pushed her forward.

Ghost Cat had committed to her swing with such certainty of hitting her target that she momentarily lost balance. Her paw swung forcefully through the air and across her body. Joonie seized the moment. He pushed the cat from behind. Her momentum was too great. She tumbled, bouncing over roots and rocks.

Joonie sprinted past the laid-out cat. When he passed her, he turned and winked.

Ghost Cat slowly got back to her feet and looked around to see if any forest creatures had seen her stumble. A few small birds sang in the branches, seemingly unaware of the incident. She watched Joonie run off, licking her paw and rubbing it across her face.

♦

Joonie looked back at Ghost Cat as she sat in the middle of the path. "When the time is right, we will run into each again," Ghost Cat called after Joonie.

"I don't see that happening anytime soon," Joonie shot back.

"You may wish it was sooner than later," Ghost Cat returned with a growl. Her body seemed to dissipate into the air.

I've got to take advantage of this lead, Joonie thought as he lengthened his stride and focused on keeping a relaxed cadence. He soon found his breath, pulling it from the tips of his paws through his legs and into his chest. He slowly blew out all the air and drew it up again. He looked back down the path. Ghost Cat was no longer there.

Joonie traveled along the path next to the stream for most of the day. He stopped occasionally to pull a long drink from the stream and eat mouthfuls of the slimy algae that grew along the banks. Joonie knew from Mother Moon that algae was a potent food source, but he could not get over the texture and gagged as it slid down his throat.

Running helped Joonie's mind relax. He focused his attention a few strides ahead of him, and his feet just found the narrow trail beneath automatically avoiding sharp rocks and impeding roots. Joonie's movements were fluid and efficient. *I wonder how Pencilthin is making out?* Joonie wondered. *He said the Confluence was three days away. But I wonder,* he chuckled, *if that's three days running like this or three days padding along on those short legs of his.* The thought of seeing Pencilthin again lifted Joonie's spirit as he continued running beside the watercourse.

Eventually the valley opened up onto the plains. Joonie saw a tall mesa in the distance. *I bet I can see the whole valley from up there. Maybe even see the Confluence.* He continued to run east, always choosing one of the deer trails that lead up out of the valley.

♦

Pencilthin sat on the shore of the Confluence soaking his paws in a shallow eddy. He had made the journey to the Confluence from the Mushroom Den in one day. He knew the shortcut between the giant oxbow that opens up at the mouth of the valley

but didn't have time to explain it to Joonie. *Following the river should only take him a couple more days,* he thought.

"What's the matter, Pencilthin?" asked one of the porcupines from the mushroom den. "You're worried about the rabbit aren't you? Do you think he'll make it here?"

"Yeah, he'll make it," Pencilthin looked up at his friend. "He's a messy, scared bunny, but he's tough. He'll make it."

Pencilthin got up and looked around at the many prairie and forest animals that had begun to assemble at the Confluence. Soup pots and a make shift kitchen were being set up. *He's tough.*

♦

Joonie had soon ascended well above the foliage of the valley floor. As the slope got steeper, he was forced to shorten his stride and focus all his energy uphill. He began chanting an ascent mantra he remembered from Father Sun:

Four legs or two?

It's up to you

As long as you continue to

Climb… climb… climb…

Chanting the mantra over and over, Joonie finally found himself out of the valley and at the base of the mesa, in a landscape of juniper and pinon pine, chokecherry bushes, prickly-pear cactus, and huge, mossy boulders. Meadowlarks and bluebirds flitted from perch to perch and sang. A Sunning lizard flicked his tongue. Far above, a hawk circled. Joonie took refuge in the shade of a sage bush.

That hawk is an issue, he thought as he looked for the best way to climb the mesa. Joonie saw little arroyos, small, dry streambeds made during the spring runoff that had a protective brush cover. When the hawk finally spiraled away from Joonie, he bolted for the nearest arroyo and dove under the overhanging brush. As he sprinted, he became vaguely aware that something was behind him. He peered out of the arroyo and thought he may have caught a glimpse of Ghost Cat.

The brush made a nice tunnel over the arroyo, so Joonie was able to climb easily to the top of the mesa. Joonie sat in the shade of the brush on the rim. The top was as flat as a table and as barren. There were only a few rocks, some sweetgrass, and sparse growths of pinon pines that offered no real protection from predators. The circling hawk had dropped lower as Joonie had climbed higher. They were now close enough to each other that when the hawk flew by, Joonie could hear the flap of his wings and see its eyes scanning the mesa-top for prey.

On the far side of the mesa-top there was a large rock outcropping. *I need to climb those rocks so I can see the Confluence,* thought Joonie. *But how do I get past that hawk?* He sat down and dug his heels in the cool sand at the mouth of the arroyo, thinking.

He watched the hawk tighten its flight pattern as it began to zero in on something toward the center of the mesa. He could see some blades of grass moving against the wind and then noticed two field mice bumbling along, carrying a large sack of dried chokecherries between them. The mice trudged forward, heads down, struggling under the weight of their burden.

When the hawk dives for the mice I'll run for the rocks, thought Joonie, preparing to bolt. The mice had stopped to take a break from carrying their heavy load. Having lost the mice in the underbrush the hawk regained some elevation his head sweeping the area thoroughly. As Joonie sat waiting, he heard the conversation of the two mice.

"How in the world are we going to get these cherries all the way down to the Confluence?" said one. "My back can't take it."

"The way to the Confluence is found one step at a time," offered the other softly.

"Oh, come off it, Meeka," said the first, sounding very irritated. "I know 'one step at a time.' Cut it out with the creepy shaman stuff. I need some real words of encouragement here."

They are going to the Confluence? thought Joonie as he watched the hawk tighten his circle once more, focusing in on the spot where the mice rested. *I've got to help them.* Recalling the attack of the hawk near the river, Joonie knew they slam into their prey with full force in an attempt to break the prey's neck. Joonie found a stout stick on the damp floor of the arroyo with a sharp end. *I think the hawk would rather have a wounded rabbit than a small mouse.*

With a lot of rustling of branches, Joonie limped a few steps to the top the mesa, holding the stout stick close to his body and out of the hawk's sight. Just as he figured, the hawk began to fly a tight circle above Joonie. Within seconds it was preparing to dive. Joonie limped a few feet more and stopped on top of a long, flat rock.

With a terrifying screech the hawk committed to its dive. The bird dropped out of the sky with such speed, Joonie barely had time to wedge the base of the stick into a crack in the rock. Still covering the stick with his body, he waited for the hawk to reach the point in its dive where it could no longer pull out. He looked up and saw the hawk knifing through the air like a lightning bolt, its golden eyes focused only on him.

When Joonie could see the tips of the bird's talons, he rolled away, leaving only the pointed stick for the hawk to slam into. The bird came down with such force that the stick pierced clean through its body. The stunned bird tried to pull itself off of the stick by flapping its wings, but its body was stuck fast. It pushed, pulled, and flapped for a long time before it finally stopped struggling and surrendered to death.

Joonie was exhilarated. *I did it! I killed a predator!* His heart swelled, and his mind tingled with adrenaline.

His excitement, though, turned to sorrow as he watched the

bird in its death throes. *I did it. I killed a predator*, he thought again, but it no longer felt like something to celebrate.

Still, Joonie turned toward the mice anticipating the same hero's recognition that Pencilthin received on the riverbank. But the mice still argued, completely unaware of what had just occurred.

"Listen, Meeka, I really am getting tired of this mystic guru stuff. I miss just talking to you."

"The me you miss never was nor will ever be again," said Meeka, beginning to shoulder the dried cherries again. "There is only the me *now*."

"Okay, that is it. You are going to take a punch in the nose if I hear that creepy tone again."

"Violence is never the answer."

That was the last straw. Eeka began chasing Meeka, shaking his small fist.

"Ah-ho!" shouted Joonie.

The mice stopped their chase and saw Joonie waving at them.

"Ah-ho yourself, rabbit!" shouted Eeka.

"Did you guys even see what just happened?" asked Joonie, a bit disappointed.

Meeka and Eeka approached Joonie and saw the impaled hawk.

"What in the world?" Meeka asked, scurrying behind Eeka.

"I just saved your fur," said Joonie, "that's what. This bird was going to snatch one of you, so I distracted him and…" Joonie stopped speaking and noticed that the mice were staring at the dead bird, their mouths and eyes open wide in disbelief.

"You killed that hawk?" asked Eeka.

"The prey does not kill the predator," said Meeka. "That changes the order of things and I… I…" he stammered, "I'm not sure if we are ready for that."

♦

The mice were significantly disturbed by the dead hawk. So, without ceremony, Joonie began walking with them across the mesa toward the rock outcropping. The mice kept a healthy distance between themselves and Joonie.

Joonie asked about the meeting at the Confluence.

"You know about the meeting?" asked Eeka.

"I don't know much," replied Joonie, "Just that some animals are gathering there to talk about bison or something, I'm really not sure."

"We don't know much, either," said Eeka. "All we have heard is that something hungry is coming from the north. Some animals have decided to meet at the Confluence to cook for them. Creatures are coming from all around to share recipes and bring ingredients. We even heard Grey, the bighorn sheep, is coming down from the high country to cook with us."

"How do you know that the hungry somethings from the north aren't predators?"

"The little birds told us," said Meeka, losing confidence in the source of information as he spoke the words aloud. Eeka gazed at the ground and kicked a pebble, suddenly remembering the lack of credibility of the news that came from small, migrating birds.

Joonie could sense the mice were eager to depart his company, so he told them he was going to climb the rock outcropping to see what he could see.

The mice grabbed their sack of dried cherries and trudged off across the mesa. Joonie could hear them argue as they went.

Joonie again sensed he was being followed. He looked around

the barren mesa. At one end was the dead bird. At the other was the first rock outcropping.

Once Joonie had learned to control his breath, running came naturally to him. Climbing steep rocks? Not so much. At the base of the outcropping he jumped from ledge to ledge, but as the rocks became steeper Joonie had to wedge himself in the cracks and inch himself up carefully.

After many scrapes and scrambles Joonie finally made it to the top of the outcropping. He looked up the Front Range from where he had come and saw in the distance the mouth of the old hole. His eyes followed the river as he focused on where he imagined the Mushroom Den to be. A surge of emotion hit Joonie as he thought of the Bedbug trace and how he led the coyotes right to them.

He brushed his tears away and let his eyes follow the valley from the south and saw below him the Confluence. Well north of the Confluence lay Cobre Canyon, a chasm that spanned the width of three mesa-tops and ran east from the base of majestic mountains as far east as Joonie could see.

Joonie's gaze continued north beyond the canyon. He saw a

brutal brown cloud billowing from the far horizon and miles up into the sky. Between the cloud and ground was a thin layer, as black as night, that stretched from the edge of the majestic mountains to the far eastern horizon.

A cold shiver ran down Joonie's spine as he watched the brown cloud billow and spew into the sky. Suddenly he felt exposed. Panic gripped his stomach. Nervously he thumped his foot and looked around. Slowly he backed under a small outcropping. He heard a clacking on the other side of a rock pillar.

I must overcome my fear. The Bedbug Trace is dead because I was afraid, Joonie thought as he began to find his breath. When he had calmed down he crawled out slowly and began to sneak around the pillar of rock.

The ledge was thin. Joonie pressed his body tightly against the rock and inched his way around. His foot hit a rotten patch of rock, which fell away as he pitched forward, almost plummeting to the sharp rocks below. Just in time he leapt forward and grasped at the slight ledge, pulling himself back up.

The clacking was getting louder and the ledge thinner, but Joonie controlled his fear. Carefully he rounded the pillar. The thin ledge ended. Joonie was at a dead end. He could not return the way he came. The ledge that crumbled left a large gap between himself and the other side. He looked ahead and saw in the distance the corner of a flat shelf of rock. If he could make the leap he should be safe. The only problem is, he would be leaping toward the source of the clacking noise.

Left without options, Joonie leapt toward the shelf. He landed on the flat rock hard, knocking the wind out him. As he looked up he saw something dark and shadowy.

It was the burnished, black, feathered form of Mal the raven.

CHAPTER NINE

The Unkindness

"Watcha doin' here, rabbit?" asked Mal. "Hunting hawks?"

Joonie looked around. He was convinced that Ghost Cat was nearby, but he nevertheless quickly turned his focus back on Mal. Noticing the raven's caution, he exhaled his fear and caught his breath. Joonie knew the sight of the impaled hawk must have made an impact on Mal. In a gesture of bravado, Joonie turned his back on the raven and stared north toward the thunderous cloud of dust and chaos.

Mal hopped to a perch closer to Joonie. "The ravens have been hearing stories about the lone rabbit and his porcupine friend. The coyotes are none too happy to have lost a member of their band to prey."

"So," said Joonie with his back still turned. "I'm none too happy with the coyotes. They killed the Bedbug Trace."

"C'mon, rabbit. Coyotes feed on rabbits. Hawks feed on rabbits. This is how it has always been. You can't wake up in a cave one day and change all that. The hawks are not going to take lightly what you did to another one of their kind, either. There will be more bloodshed."

"Mal, I am truly not interested in how the coyotes or hawks

feel about my actions." Looking toward the impressive cloud on the northern horizon Joonie shivered. He looked around him again for Ghost Cat. "Times have changed."

Noticing Joonie's preoccupation with the northern horizon, Mal said, "The ravens have information about the Harbinger Stampede." Joonie's ear perked up. "Yes, lots of information."

Joonie looked up and saw an entire unkindness of ravens spiraling above him. One large bird detached from the group and landed on the perch next to Mal. The raven was much bigger than Mal and had feathers so lustrous they looked like rainbows. His beak was as black as obsidian and was as sharp as an arrow. Unlike Mal, Joonie sensed no fear in him.

"Goyo, this is the lone rabbit I told you about," said Mal, bobbing and bowing as he spoke.

"The great rabbit hunter," Goyo said, laughing. He sized Joonie up and down. "Tell me, rabbit, why are you here?"

"That's a good question," said Joonie. "I'd be happy to tell you if you give me some information first."

"Fair enough," clacked Goyo. "You want to know about the Harbinger Stampede, don't you?"

"Indeed," said Joonie.

"The bison are stampeding south, trampling everything in their path. They have destroyed countless dens, warrens, and nests. Entire collectives of animals have been wiped out. The dust they have kicked up has blocked the Sun, and the prairie left behind is a lifeless desert littered with the carcasses of bison, antelope, and every other prairie dweller."

Joonie again looked north to the great approaching storm. He focused on the thin, black line between the dust and earth and realized that eternal black strip was hundreds of thousands, if not millions, of stampeding bison heading south.

"Never have we ravens heard of destruction like this," continued Goyo. "We have flown over the stampede, but we cannot see what is happening. The invaders operate beneath the cover of the brown cloud. We only know what we were told by a small prairie dog who died after she retold what she had witnessed." Joonie's brow furrowed. "She collapsed beneath our tree," Goyo continued. "One of our unkindness thought a meal had been delivered and flew down to feast on the dying creature. When he arrived she was muttering to herself. She held up a paw to our raven and looked at him with eyes that held him still. Before her last breath she described to him the birth of the hideous monsters and their brutality. We know what the stampede is a harbinger of, and I can tell you this: As destructive as the bison are, they are nothing compared to the Iam that feed off of them."

The Iam. Joonie almost slipped from the rock when he heard Goyo speak the name. In a flash the pieces of Joonie's life began to fit together. Joonie recalled the stories of the Iam trying to settle on the earth's surface, and how Runners were chosen to keep them from doing so. Ghost Cat's words came flooding into his memory: "A rabbit is a strange choice for a Runner."

No, I can't be a Runner, Joonie thought, knowing as well as he knew anything that he indeed was. Joonie's mind raced. The responsibility crashed down upon him. He felt like throwing up. *I'm just a rabbit.*

With his head cocked sideways Goyo stared deep into Joonie's eyes.

Standing on the top of the mesa, Joonie looked from the stampede in the north, past Cobre Canyon, to the Confluence below him.

Accepting his fate, he immediately began calculating.

"You know of the Iam?" asked Goyo with a nod of encouragement.

All too aware of the implication his next few words would have, Joonie took a deep breath and attempted to regain his composure.

"Never heard of 'em," he said. "But they must be pretty bad to scare the bison like that." He nodded toward the tremendous dust cloud.

"We have not yet the words to explain the depth of their evil," Goyo paused studying Joonie. "If the Runner fails to stop the Iam they will teach us an entire new vocabulary in which to describe cruelty," said Goyo darkly. "They are fueled solely by their enormous, unquenchable appetites. They won't stop until they consume everything on the surface, and when the earth is left a dry desert they will travel up to the next surface and do the same to it."

"Nothing can stop them?" asked Joonie innocently.

"Only a Runner," answered Goyo. He cocked his head closer and watched for a response.

Joonie feigned ignorance, "A Runner? What's a Runner?"

Goyo laughed. "A Runner, Joonie, is a creature chosen by fate and raised by the Sun and the Moon to stop the Iam!" Having had enough of games, Goyo grew angry. "Enough of this playfulness, Joonie. I know who you are and why you are here! Now I need to know if you have a plan."

Joonie again scanned the expanse of land between the Harbinger Stampede, Cobre Canyon, and the Confluence. In his head he had quickly roughed out a course of action. As ill-conceived as it was, it depended heavily on the role Goyo would play.

"If you are suggesting that the Runner is me, you are mistaken. But you are right in thinking I have something to do with the plan. I will tell you the plan, but it's too late. It is already well into action."

Goyo ruffled his feathers and hopped closer to Joonie. "The porcupine," breathed Goyo, guessing that the spined animal who kills coyotes must be the Runner. "Tell me everything, rabbit, and I will tell you if it's too late or not."

Joonie confessed as if he had nothing to lose. "The prey have banded together. They have learned the secrets to defeating the predators."

Goyo looked to the rim of the mesa and saw the upright stick in the ground that pinned the dead hawk.

"You see, this is true," said Joonie.

Goyo nodded. "And where did the prey learn to do this?"

"From the Iam."

"Impossible. The Iam don't negotiate with any creature."

"You know that the Iam have tried to consume this surface many times in the past," said Joonie. "But they've always been pushed back by a Runner. They are trying a different tact."

"The prey are fools to negotiate with the Iam."

"We have faith the Runner with stop the Iam again. And when they are gone we will still have the knowledge of how to kill predators," bluffed Joonie.

"And if the Runner does not stop the Iam?"

"Then the hunters and the hunted shall share the same fate."

Goyo hopped back and thought about what Joonie had said. He too had begun his calculations.

CHAPTER TEN

The Confluence

Grey, the big horn sheep, walked among the prairie animals at the Confluence of the Aquacita River and Blossom Creek, examining the preparations for the feast.

Prairie animals from the surrounding area arrived carrying loads of regional ingredients with which to prepare dishes and drinks to share amongst themselves and the guests approaching from the north. These gatherings of prairie animals were common but were usually held on either side of the Front Range. This was the first time anyone remembered having a feast at the Confluence, usually animals just migrated past to the other side of the valley.

An unfamiliar tension hung in the air, however, as the animals relayed rumors about the Harbinger Stampede.

A young prong-horned antelope spoke in a foreboding tone as he absently prepared to light the pyramid of wood for the soup fire. “We heard about huge, rolling heads with wide, gaping mouths coming this way, eating everything in their path.”

Grey appeared in a flash, extinguishing the flame. “I told everyone, no fires are to be lit until the rabbit arrives.”

“Sorry,” the antelope said, rolling his eyes.

Pencilthin noticed Grey’s agitation and approached him in

hopes to calm him down. "Grey, why don't we just light a fire or two just to get things started? It may be a day or two before Joonie gets here."

"No," Grey shot back. "The fires are lit when the rabbit arrives. End of story."

"Sorry Grey," Pencilthin said, rolling his eyes.

A squirrel picked up where the antelope left off. "We heard the same, only the heads were being pushed by hairless creatures with big legs and feet."

The smaller, furry animals sat in a circle that began to tighten as the stories continued. Little pups hung around their parents, listening until they could take no more before dashing away and reporting what they had just heard to the other little ones scampering about.

Around a stump, a covey of ptarmigan prepared vegetables for the soup and discussed the wisdom of the plan to cook for the unknown visitors.

"I know Grey thinks this offering is the right thing to do, but I think the old goat might be crazy," said one.

A few birds bobbed their heads in agreement.

"Grey is a bighorn sheep, not a mountain goat," corrected another. "Anyway, whatever it is that's coming it's pure evil. I can feel it in the hollows of my bones."

The covey, chopping squash, shucking beans, and dekerneling-corn, bobbed their heads in agreement.

♦

Joonie scaled down the steep side of the mesa and headed toward the Confluence. Once he hit flat ground he began running and following the contours of the land. He expected to arrive at the Confluence in a day, just in time to meet Pencilthin.

As he ran Joonie meditated on the plan he had rapidly hatched on the mesa-top. He was so lost in thought he hardly noticed the scampering of animals around him until he almost bumped into one.

A rabbit.

"Ah-ho," said Joonie.

The bunny scuttled off wordlessly. As Joonie looked around, he noticed hundreds of young rabbits dashing about.

I must be in one of the outer rings of the Red Earth Trace, Joonie thought.

He jumped in front of an oncoming rabbit. "Ah-ho," he said.

"Ah-ho," returned the rabbit, anxiously thumping his foot and looking well beyond Joonie.

"Are you Red Earth Trace?" asked Joonie.

"We are," the rabbit replied.

"Where is the warren?"

The rabbit pointed east and scurried away.

"Perfect, I was heading that..." Joonie watched as the rabbit disappeared into the shadows of the bushes before he could finish his sentence.

The outer ring of Red Earth Trace was made up of hundreds of adolescent and very old rabbits scurrying about, nervously eating the grasses and dashing back and forth from the cover of the surrounding chokecherry and dogwood bushes. Silently they went about their routine, constantly looking around and above them for predators that were never far away.

Joonie became aware that he was entering the next ring of the trace. He felt the tension in the rabbits fade away. Insulated by the fodder of rabbits that were too young or too old to breed, the second ring was populated by rabbits courting each other with playful histrionics. A trio of males wrestled around vying for the attention of a beautiful female. As Joonie approached, she bounded right up to him, much to the chagrin of the males who eyed Joonie jealously.

"Ah-ho," she said in the softest, dreamiest voice Joonie had ever heard.

"Ahhh…." Joonie's reply stuck in his throat and sounded very much like a sneeze.

The female laughed. "Would YOU like to graze?" she asked, staring into Joonie's eyes.

Joonie felt hot. He began to pant. At that moment grazing with her was all he desired.

She took his paw and led him to the tender, young grasses that grew near a small tributary stream. As he nibbled the leaves of grass, she gently stroked his head with her soft ears. Inside the rings of the trace, Joonie was no longer a lone rabbit. He felt part of something bigger than himself. He knew the security that a trace offers. He even almost forgot about the dust cloud, the stampeding bison, the Confluence, the approaching Iam…

Joonie jumped up, startling the doe. "I… I have to go," Joonie

stammered. They were the most difficult words he had ever spoken. She looked at Joonie as if he were crazy.

"What?" she said.

"I have to go! Now!" Joonie said and sprinted off.

The female shook her head and pranced off to rejoin the trio of males who were now giving attention to a slightly less attractive female.

♦

A nurse mother greeted Joonie at the perimeter of the Warren, the nucleus of Red Earth Trace. She promptly grabbed him by the ear and twisted.

"Oh, no, you don't," she scolded. "You get yourself back into the outer rings. You should be ashamed of yourself, bounding in here like some kind of privileged prince."

Joonie laughed.

"Oh, you think this is funny, do you? We'll see how funny you think it is when I take you to the admonishment circle." She started dragging Joonie toward the center of the Warren.

Admonishment circle? Joonie laughed even harder. He went along with her passively. He was completely subdued by a sense of security. The Warren was like rabbit heaven for Joonie. He felt as if he'd returned to something completely familiar. From the mouths of cozy, little holes dug into the side hills, mama bunnies tended house as their newborn kittens learned to hop. Nurse Mothers strolled the soft grasses, holding the hands of pregnant rabbits, helping them through their birth process. Cook fires smoldered as the soup simmered and steamed.

On a nearby mound, rabbits gathered round to watch a play. The performers wore costumes. Some were outfitted in masks of hideous monsters, and others were dressed as bison. Joonie imagined this was the retelling of the Harbinger Stampede.

As the monsters began overtaking the bison, a rabbit dressed beautifully in robes of silver and white slowly danced an arc around the characters. She rattled a stick adorned with bells and feathers: *toe, toe,step… toe, toe, step.* Four rabbits with soft mallets began beating a large drum. *DUM, DUM, dum, dum… DUM, DUM, dum, dum… DUM, DUM, dum, dum.*

From the other side of the arena a rabbit dressed in robes of orange, yellow, and red also began to dance an arc around the performers who were still in conflict. The dancer mumbled chants as he danced: *toe, toe, step…toe, toe, step.* The two dancers followed each other in a circle, and the drummers began to pick up the tempo. *DUM, DUM, dum, dum… DUM, DUM, dum, dum.*

Beyond the elliptical dancers Joonie noticed a dancer painted with black and white horizontal stripes and a big red grin that harassed the other dancers by poking and pushing them.

"Who is that?" Joonie asked a nearby rabbit.

"That's the clown," the rabbit replied.

"But it's not funny,"

"Yeah, that's exactly the point," the rabbit concluded leaving Joonie bewildered.

The rabbit in the white robes, whom Joonie figured represented Mother Moon, danced a smaller circle inside where the red rabbit danced. As the tempo increased, the two dancers began to catch up with each other. The beat reached a frenzy as the white rabbit began to eclipse the red Sun rabbit. The bison and the monsters jumped up and down. Dust rose from their feet. Joonie became woozie as the two dancers reached for each others hand.

Joonie looked around at the other rabbits in the warren. They gently swayed. They seemed to be floating. The bison and monster rabbits halted their chase and swayed, anticipating the connection being made between the orbiting dancers. At the very moment the tips of the dancers paws delicately touched, the heads of the warren rabbits snapped toward the north in unison. The spell was broken as the scent of blood, fear, and predators filled the air. "COYOTES!" the collective alarm was cried.

In a flash, a band of coyotes tore into the Warren. Their mugs were bloody, and their eyes were filled with rage. They barked and growled as the mothers gathered their young and scampered off into their holes.

Joonie tore away from the Nurse Mother and began running through the Warren. The largest of the coyotes gave chase. They had followed Joonie into the trace, and he led them directly to the Warren. The alpha coyote, Grub, growled as he quickly gained on Joonie. He could feel the pounding of Grub's paws behind him. Running as fast he could, he looked ahead of him and saw he was running straight for Ghost Cat, who was crouched down ready to strike with a look of hatred on her face.

Betray your instincts, Joonie heard Pencilthin saying. *I will not be afraid. I will not run. I will not hide.* Joonie looked straight into Ghost Cat's green eyes.

"I told you when the time was right we'd run into each other again," growled Ghost Cat. Joonie felt the power of the hatred in Ghost Cat's eyes. Although she was speaking to him, he noticed that the glare was not directed at him, but at Grub. So with the coyote immediately behind him and the Ghost Cat in front, Joonie stopped right in front of the mighty feline. He recalled Father Sun's advice: *Give your fear a name. Ghost Cat is my fear, and I must face it.* Joonie exhaled, and with that breath went his fear. *I leave my fear here.*

Claws out and fangs bared, Ghost Cat sprang at Joonie. Calmly he faced her. Joonie closed his eyes and drew a deep breath up from his paws. In that breath, Joonie was filled with serenity. He raised a paw to the attacking cat and exhaled slowly. Joonie stared into the green eyes of the cat allowing for what came next. Ghost Cat dissipated into a thin mist. Joonie breathed the mist in. With that breath he absorbed all the power of Ghost Cat. He was no longer afraid.

The coyote recognized the shift in Joonie from scared rabbit

to dominant animal and abruptly skidded to a stop on his heels. Calmly Joonie raised his paw to the baffled Grub, who tucked his tail between his legs and began shaking.

The other coyotes in the band stopped pillaging and bore witness to their leader cowering before a bunny. Joonie gently placed his paw on the snout of the big dog and stared directly into his eyes, pushing his head into the dirt.

Joonie left the cowering coyote in the dirt and walked up to another coyote, who held a pregnant rabbit by her ear. As he got closer, the coyote dropped the bunny and ran from the Warren.

Joonie returned to the trembling Grub. "The tables have turned, dog," Joonie said, placing his foot on its muzzle. "The prey is becoming the predator." The coyote closed his eyes and whimpered. "Gather the predators north of the dust cloud, and the prey will settle this once and for all."

The usurped coyote got up and began backing away from Joonie. Then he turned tail and ran.

The Warren was silent but for the cries of the young bunnies. Joonie looked around to see hundreds of eyes staring at him in disbelief.

"I have to go," he said and ran away from the Warren toward the Confluence.

♦

The little birds arrived at the Confluence before Joonie and had already begun telling their version of the coyotes-in-the-Warren story.

"Joonie is a coyote killer, he is," they chirped. "Joonie said we are going after the hunters. He did say. Joonie is on his way. He is. We like bees. We do." The little birds' attention span is flightly at best.

Pencilthin heard the news and ran it through his small, migrating bird filter. *Joonie is alive,* he thought. As he looked about the Confluence he noticed Grey nervously adjusting the soup fire fuel preparing them for ignition.

The news from the small, migrating birds—combined with Meeka and Eeka Mouse telling of their encounter with Joonie and how he killed the hawk on the mesa-top—created an exhilarating environment around the Confluence. The animals were beginning to accept that their lives were changing. *A rabbit that kills hawks and can intimidate coyotes? What is going on?* the animals asked Pencilthin. But the porcupine had no answers.

"We will wait for Joonie," he said.

♦

As Joonie ran toward the Confluence he thought again of his plan. He considered the distance between the stampede and the canyon, the speed at which the bison were running, and the brown cloud of dust that hid the Iam's maneuvering from view. Joonie hoped Goyo and Grub would succeed in gathering the predators north of the stampede.

When Joonie entered the Confluence, the animals were waiting silently for him. Each reverently patted Joonie on the back and nodded encouragement as he passed. When Joonie neared the meeting place of the two rivers, Pencilthin greeted him with a delicate hug, which is how all porcupines hug.

The silence was broken by a loud clatter and yelling that came from behind a large cottonwood tree where the animals were doing their cooking. A humiliated squirrel came sulking out of the makeshift kitchen followed by some more curses. Then came another loud crash of pots followed by a set of squirrels bounding out of the kitchen. Chasing them was a rabbit followed by two little bunnies scampering at her apron string, wielding a spoon.

It was Bedbug, the Cook Bunny, and her even smaller Bedbug trace.

Grey, the big horn sheep, began to light the soup fires.

CHAPTER ELEVEN

The Contracting Stampede

Grub lay awake and shivering under the cold, night sky. He was outside the circle of snuggled, sleeping coyotes.

He had expected to lose his alpha status when he was whipped by a rabbit. Actually, he expected the rest of the band to tear his limbs off and leave his carcass for the magpies to pick apart. After all, that was exactly what he did to Thrush, the alpha before him.

But they let Grub live. They even allowed him to sleep near the band. Grub knew why. They were scared. That and the fact that nothing had stepped into the alpha roll by beating Grub except a dumb bunny. And they weren't about to go follow that morsel.

The world is going all topsy-turvy, thought Grub as he inched closer to the band for warmth. *The rabbit told me to gather my forces north of Cobre Canyon, but those dogs will tear my throat out if I so much make a low growl.*

Grub heard one coyote let out a loud, high-pitched fart in the face of another coyote, who in turn growled and snapped at the sleeping gas-passer. The rest of the band, half awake, shifted around, scratched the ground, and settled in for sleep. The flatulent coyote, desperate to regain status in the band, saw Grub sneaking closer to the band. The newly disgraced coyote lunged toward Grub, baring his teeth and releasing a torrent of barks that drove Grub back.

Unable to sleep, Grub, tossed and turned. He remembered the whooping he took from the rabbit. Lying on his back he looked up into the branches and saw the silhouette of a raven.

"Hello, birdie," grumbled Grub.

The Raven silently glided to the ground next to Grub.

"Oh, Goyo," said Grub, startled to see *the* Goyo, "I'm sorry. I thought it was that poncie, Mal."

"Grub, so nice to see you," said Goyo. "I hear your nose will be stuck in dog butts for awhile. It must be difficult to lose the view from the front of the pack." The raven laughed.

Grub said nothing. He knew the entire valley had heard about his defeat at the paws of a rabbit.

"Tell me," said Goyo, "after the rabbit dominated you, did he say anything?"

"Dominated? Ouch." He avoided Goyo's stare. "Yes, he did say something to me. Grub had repeated Joonie's words a thousand times since he said them. 'Gather the predators north of the dust cloud, and the prey will settle this once and for all.' He didn't consider the fact that I wouldn't be able to gather lice after he stood on my nose."

Goyo hopped silently around the sleeping coyote band. He went up close to a sleeping dog's ear and whispered something. He didn't stir. "Pretty sound sleepers, eh?"

"I guess it depends on the type of noise you make." Grub recalled.

Goyo hopped around and around the circle, whispering a secret to each coyote, over and over again throughout the night. As the Sun began to rise, Goyo hopped back over to Grub, who had fallen asleep, and woke him up.

"When the band awakens, you will once more be the alpha," Goyo said as Grub stretched. "Take the band north of the dust cloud." And with that, Goyo flew from the coyotes and headed north.

♦

The coyote band woke up and began piecing together their collective dream.

"We were tearing through the fodder circle of a trace and then through the breeders," started one.

"We entered the Warren," said another.

A third joined the story. "A rabbit shoved Grub's nose in the dirt."

Seizing the moment, Grub jumped into center of the circle. "Enough of this silly dream!" he barked, spitting foam on the muzzle of the latest dreamweaver. The coyotes didn't have time to separate their dream from reality before Grub commanded, "Follow me!" and loped off.

The band followed Grub through the foothills, heading north as if the defeat Grub had suffered by a rabbit was but a dream. As they trotted through the foothills, Grub shook his head in further disgrace. He knew that was not the first time Goyo had influenced a coyote band's dreams.

♦

Hundreds of Alooshi bounded across the prairie, their long, thin legs loping around the bison obstinacy. They ran to the far eastern horizon and west to the base of the foothills. When they reached the outskirts of the stampede, they formed a perimeter around the herd. The Wadi banged their clubs and gnashed their terrible teeth, nipping at the heels of the bison, pushing them relentlessly forward as the Alooshi forcing them inward.

Many bison were crushed to death or suffocated in the mayhem. Their bodies were carried along for miles, squeezed between their charging mates. They were packed so tightly together, smaller bison were popped up from the ground and continued running on the back of the herd. Or they were trampled deep into the earth by thousands of hooves.

The Tar-Reefs were complaining to the Overseer that they had nothing to inspect. The bison had trampled every living thing on the prairie to dust. That dust now clogged the noses and ears of the floppy beasts, leaving them without their senses.

"The dust will clear soon enough, and you can freely account for everything on this beautiful surface," said the Overseer, whose crimson robe snapped in a strong burst of wind. The Tar-Reefs struggled against the gale, wiping their goggles with strips of white sheets as they plodded behind the Overseer, who followed the Wadi, who followed the bison, and who are surrounded by

Alooshi. All of them caught up in a mad rush toward the North Rim of Cobre Canyon.

♦

The mood at the Confluence was somber as hundreds more prairie animals began to arrive. They told horror stories of what was happening to the boroughs, lodges, hives, and warrens of their families on the north side of the canyon. Each arriving animal had heard they should bring food to cook. Soon, stacks of beans, corn, squash, greens, berries, and roots began to amass near the Confluence.

The smoke from the soup fires streamed up through the warm air of the valley in long black ribbons until it became trapped under the ceiling of cold air that drifted over from the tall mountains.

Pencilthin followed the ribbons of smoke until it flattened under the temperature inversion of the valley. He had never seen smoke fail to disappear into the blue sky above.

♦

On the soft sandbar dotted with smooth river rocks and rounded driftwood, Bedbug and Joonie stared at the blending of the two rivers. The water from the Aquacita was cloudy with silt loosened from a high country storm, while the water from Blossom Creek was clear and green. At the Confluence the two waters met, swirling into each other like two spirits, neither yielding, combining then moving on as a deeper and calmer water flow.

Joonie could sense that Bedbug needed to talk about the events that had unfolded since they last saw each other on that terrible night.

"The coyotes were just mad with blood. After they ripped us from tree…" Bedbug stared weakly out at the married waters. Her voice trembled as she gathered the strength to continue.

Joonie shifted uncomfortably on the sand. He knew what she told next was a result of his panic. He closed his eyes and took Bedbug's paw in his, and she resumed.

"After they ripped us from the tree it was a frenzy. The coyotes were out of control. They didn't want to eat us. They kept barking, 'Know your place, rabbits, know you place.' The two youngest bunnies in our trace died of fright. Two others didn't survive the puncture wounds. Only myself and these two little ones survived." She nodded her head toward the small puffballs that sat at her side. "The coyotes could not kill us all. It is against their code to kill an entire trace. But they reduced us down to almost nothing." Bedbug hid her eyes behind her ears as she started to sob.

"I am so very sorry," Joonie said, knowing that the words could not begin to make the horrible situation better.

"We knew our place, Joonie. Rabbits live in order to keep other predators fed. It's an honored position in the cycle of life. We respected that, that is, until you and Pencilthin showed up." Bedbug's ear went back, and there was anger in her eyes.

"And you are okay with that position?" Joonie asked his own ire rising. "You don't mind living your life as a meal?"

"Being a meal is only a moment, an opportunity to be reborn. The joy of living is being part of a trace, being part something bigger than oneself. But you are a lone rabbit, Joonie. You wouldn't know anything about that."

Pencilthin, had joined the couple on the banks of the Confluence, and at last he interjected, "Hey, Bedbug put down your dukes. That ain't fair."

"And you, porcupine, are no better. We prey were content with our lot in life until you started reversing the roles." Bedbug looked down at one of the small bunnies of the trace. "This little one here talks about how she's going to poke a badger in the eye."

Pencilthin nudged the small bunny. "All right, just remember the power comes from your legs, so square up and RWAHHH!" he yelled, sending the bunny tumbling tip over tail.

Bedbug was furious. "I'm serious. You two are sending our world into turmoil."

"Please understand, Bedbug," Joonie implored. "Just as you were born into this world, a part of trace, I was born into this world alone. I didn't choose to be a lone rabbit, but that's how it is, and there is no sense moping about it. I've been bumbling around trying to figure out how I, a lone rabbit, fit into this crazy world." Joonie dug his heels into the damp sand of the riverbank. He took a deep breath and continued. "I have to believe I am a part of something bigger than myself, and so I play my part, even if it hasn't been played before. I play it because there *is* something bigger than traces, dens, prickles, coteries, and obstinacies, something that even, I, a lone rabbit, am a part of."

"What is it?" asked Bedbug.

"Soup," answered Joonie, throwing a stone into the swirling waters.

Pencilthin blinked, "Soup? Why does that make sense?"

Bedbug nodded, remembering Joonie's comment about soup being something unique unto itself, more than just a sum of its ingredients. "It does make sense," she said. She, Pencilthin and Joonie grasped hands. Their laughter and sorrow swirled together, combining and becoming something bigger and deeper than what it was when separated.

♦

Grey was the organizer of the cooking operation. By his side was Bedbug, giving direction and keeping animals motivated.

"Someone stomp those berries and put the juice in the open jars," she commanded. "I have a feeling we are going to need a lot of wine."

Two beavers stomped on an abundance of raspberries in a woven basket with a spigot on the bottom, which flowed into wide mouth clay jars. A prickle of porcupines ground dried corn with a tiny bit of ash in a concave stone. Countless squirrels, chipmunks, mice, and other smaller animals shucked beans out of their husks. Others peeled burdock and cut up squash. Grey kept a notebook filled with recipes of all the regional delights.

"Why are you writing all this down?" asked a precocious little squirrel. "We all know the recipes."

Grey continued writing. "Well, what if the visitors want to make these dishes? They don't have the recipe memorized like us."

The little Squirrel looked at a Grey. "Haven't you heard? The creatures approaching from the north don't want to eat *with* us, they want to eat *us*."

A number of animals, including Joonie and Pencilthin, had gathered around Grey—and the vocal little squirrel who had dared to ask the question that was on everyone's mind.

Grey looked around at the faces of the prairie animals and sighed. "Yes, I know the stories. And I believe them to be true." The animals whispered among themselves until an antelope spoke

aloud. "Then why are we still cooking all this food? We should be running south."

"That is a good thought, antelope, and you should follow through on it if you believe it the right course of action," said Grey.

The antelope looked around. None of the animals moved, so he stayed put as well.

Grey spoke again. "Friends, I know many of you think I have slipped and have grown soft-brained. After all those years above the tree line, I can tell you that I have slipped a thousand times, and I know trying to convince others of your sanity is a losing battle. If I *were* to try and convince you I'm not crazy, what I have to say next will convince of the exact opposite. You will think I am crazier than you might have imagined." More animals had gathered round Grey.

Grey closed his eyes. "One cold, clear morning, I climbed high on top of Big Black Mountain. I wanted to look out over the expanse of land before the winter snow came. As the early morning Sun warmed me, I experienced the clearest head I have ever had the fortune to possess. At that moment I was aware of everything and everything was perfect, except one thing.

"In the next moment it was as if I had been skinned alive. I was overcome with anxiety and fear. I saw the future, and it was ugly. I wanted to run as fast as I could and throw myself off the mountainside. I could not bear the thought of the future." Grey opened his eyes. "And then I heard it, or I should say, I felt it. In that darkest moment I received a message: 'Gather all the peaceful creatures at the Confluence, and cook the food of the valley and keep the recipes.' The voice was so clear and direct; I recognized it as a command, not a suggestion. I knew I had to follow through. Being given this job has helped pull me out of my misery." Grey decided to leave off another detail he received in the message: *Don't start the fires until the Runner arrives.*

A few animals nodded in support, while others shook their heads in confusion. "But here we are. The animals have gathered. The food has been cooked, and I have documented all the recipes." Grey paused and looked around. "For what, though? A terrible storm is coming, and I have no idea what to do." Grey was choked with tears.

"Well," said Joonie quietly, "I have a plan."

The animals parted and gave Joonie space. "The bison are heading straight toward Cobre Canyon, he said, "which is a dead end. There is no way to cross. The bison are being chased by the Iam."

The animals began to chatter and shuffle. "The Iam," they whispered. "Goodness."

Joonie continued. "Some of us will go to the south rim and wait for the bison to reach the far edge. Having reached the dead end, they will have no choice but to turn back north, charging right back into the Iam. I think the Iam will have to turn and run north, where hopefully they will find a legion of unhappy predators waiting to drive them back into the hole from which they came."

A number of prairie dogs, who had heard first hand the accounts of Zero's story, filled in the animals about the beasts and the hole.

"How do you know there will be an army of predators waiting for the them?" asked Pencilthin.

"I don't know if they will be there or not," replied Joonie. The animals shuffled back and forth, their concern growing. "We can only hope. Everything has been set in motion. The rest is up to fate."

The animals were confused. Joonie was a rabbit. What did he

know about the Iam, stampeding bison, and legions of waiting predators? Uneasiness began to take hold of the animals.

"The antelope are heading south," said the prong-horn, who realized running was indeed the best course of action. "We are sorry, rabbit, but relying on fate doesn't give us a lot of confidence."

A menagerie of prairie dwellers sided with the antelope and departed in a quiet mass migration south. A hollow knot of abandonment filled Joonie. He was afraid to turn around and face those that stayed. *I am such an idiot! We should all go.* From that moment on the mesa top, when he accepted he was a Runner, Joonie allowed his confidence to blossom. He imagined the success of his plan. He even visualized the reception he would receive when the Iam were turned back at the canyon's edge to be mauled by the awaiting predators. The thought of being a hero carried Joonie, distracted him from what was really going on. Joonie's confidence fled like the antelope. *I'm just a rabbit, and a rabbit is a strange choice for a Runner after all.*

Joonie slowly revolved on his heels. Bedbug and Pencilthin remained. "We're standing by you, Joonie," said Bedbug.

Grey, the big-horn sheep, and a group of animals, mostly small burrowers, surrounded the soup pots and stacks of food. "We will be here waiting for your return," he said

The heartache Joonie felt from the animals fleeing and losing hope was far greater than the gratitude he felt from the support of those that remained.

Pencilthin attempted to fill Joonie's hollowness. "It hurts terribly when critters turn their back on you," said the porcupine. "But it's important to focus on those who haven't. We stayed because our hearts are with you. We believe in your vision." He stopped and put his arm around Joonie. "That, and nobody else had a better plan." He slapped Joonie on the back.

Joonie shook his head at Pencilthin as his breath returned.

With his two friends by his side, Joonie resisted the urge to yell at the top his lungs to the remaining animals, *Run for your lives!* But he had to say something. "Well," he began his address, but he was interrupted by one of the bouncing Bedbug Trace.

"Are you the Runner?" the little one squeaked.

"Um, that's a good question. I'm pretty sure that I am the Runner."

"Pretty sure?" the bunny shot back.

"To be honest I'm not sure of anything. I'm dealing with a whole lot of new information and trying to make sense of it."

"Well, were you raised by the Sun and the Moon?" another little animal asked.

"Yes," Joonie answered confidently.

An excitement swept up through the crowd with this news.

"Well then, you are the Runner," the little bunny concluded.

As simple as that, thought Joonie.

The animals did not seem to need any more assurance. They disbanded and returned to the task of preparing the gathered food.

♦

From the north side of the canyon came a distant rumble.

"It sounds like a storm is rolling in," said Bedbug, eyeing the darkening sky.

"That's what I thought," said Porcupine. "But the noise is not like any storm I've ever heard. It's just a constant rumble."

In the time they were talking, the noise grew louder.

"That's no storm," came a dry and raspy voice from what looked like a stump of petrified wood.

"Who said that?" asked Pencilthin, looking around him.

"That's the sound of the stampede," came the voice again.

Pencilthin walked over to the gnarly brown stump and begin searching around for the source of the commentary. As Pencilthin examined the stump, it began to move in a long, slow motion. The stump advanced slightly forward and stopped again.

Joonie walked around the stump, peering underneath it, when a wizened old head that looked like a dried-up apple emerged.

"Grandfather Tortoise," gasped Pencilthin.

"It is my understanding that there is a Runner present," the old Tortoise wheezed as small white butterflies fluttered around his head.

Joonie stared at the ancient creature before him. *Wow. Now I understand why the little birds thought he may have been dead.* Grandfather Tortoise's giant, peeling shell was covered in colorful lichen on the side that faces south. The northern side of his shell was mossy. Bunches of mushrooms and small ferns sprouted amid the green moss.

Pencilthin and Bedbug stepped back, leaving only Joonie in the presence of the most respected of all the high-desert plateau creatures.

Grandfather Tortoise slowly opened one eye. The eye was covered with an opaque cataract that swirled like a cloud. He studied Joonie. His hooked mouth creaked open. "A rabbit is a strange choice for a Runner," he said, closing his eye and inhaling deeply. "But, I suppose, so was a Tortoise."

"You are the Runner?" Joonie asked, his eyes following what looked like a small fly that was buzzing around the reptile's shell.

Grandfather closed his eye and blew up a dust cloud as he released a deep breath. "No, rabbit. I *was* a Runner. You are the Runner now."

The small fly that circled Grandfather Tortoise began to circle faster around his shell. Joonie stepped back as the fly grew to the size of a skipping stone and began spinning on its axis as it continued its orbit.

When Grandfather Tortoise laughed, the orbiting disk turned from gray to a fiery orange. The disk expanded its circuit, encircling Joonie.

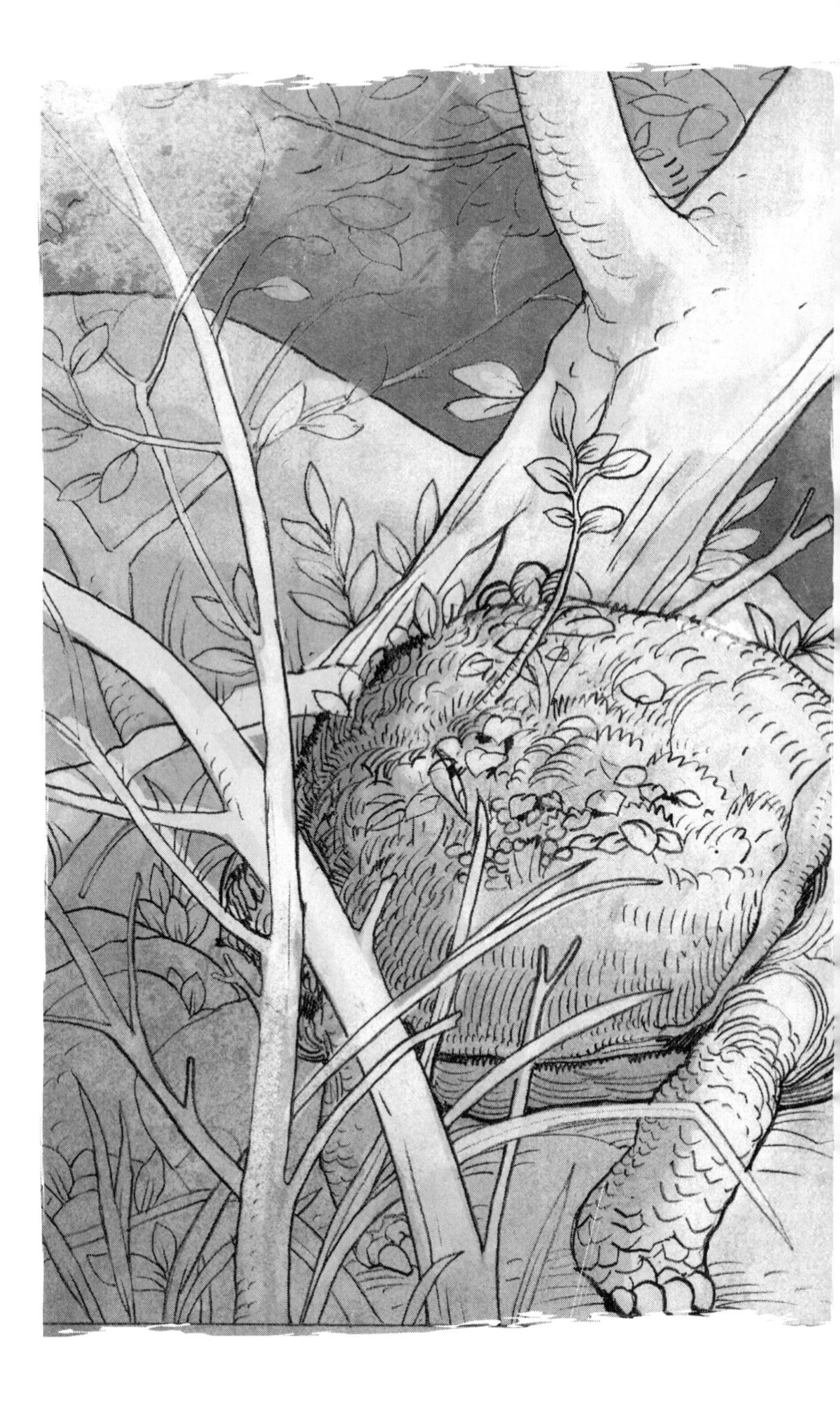

"What is this thing?" Joonie stammered. The disk, now fluttering near his face, emitted a soft hum and turned bright pink.

Grandfather said nothing. Joonie thought he had fallen asleep. Then he opened his cloudy eye again and let out a huge puff of breath as if he had be holding it for minutes. "Oh, she likes you," he responded, watching the dancing, orbiting stone. "That is a Watchi Stone."

"What does it do," Joonie asked warily.

"Many things," rasped Tortoise. "But the one thing critters find most interesting is this." He closed his eyes again as the stone returned to a tight orbit around his shell. Within seconds it was speeding around. Grandfather Tortoise snapped open his eye looking directly at a large boulder that was near the group. The stone flew from the shell, smashing the huge boulder into dust.

Joonie, Bedbug, and Pencilthin ducked and covered their heads as the rock dust settled on top of them.

The Watchi Stone then returned to a lazy circle around Grandfather Tortoise.

"We battle the Iam for our very nature," Grandfather said.

"But you won, right?" asked Joonie.

The tempest in Tortoise's eye swirled. "I suppose it depends on who you ask." He laughed a dry, wheezy laugh.

"Time is leaving me, Rabbit. Is there anything you want to ask me?"

Joonie's mind raced with a thousand questions, but it sounded as if Grandfather Tortoise was looking to answer only one. Like silt in still water, Joonie allowed the chatter in his head to settle until there was one clear question remained. Joonie made sure Bedbug and Pencilthin were out of earshot as he leaned in close to Grandfather Tortoise.

"There are so many questions," Joonie said.

"Don't worry. There are no secrets. Everything is accessible except one thing. That one thing can only be perceived by two things which renders the one thing unperceivable." Tortoise's rheumy eyes glowed with joy as he began to laugh. "Isn't that hilarious?" he gasped. Joonie gave Tortoise a blank look.

Tortoise coughed and spit as he regained composure. "Now that's what I call comedy."

The humor was completely lost on Joonie. He waited patiently for Tortoise to settle back down before he asked his question.

Joonie looked again to make sure Bedbug and Pencilthin were far enough away.

"Can I choose *not* to be the Runner?" he whispered.

Tortoise returned to his dry laughter and slowly nodded his head. "Fate and Choice are battling as we speak." Tortoise's voice began to rise. "Even if you choose not to *be* the Runner, the battle with the Iam will come to you. This is your moment. The stage has been set by many unseen forces. Don't turn your back now. Charge forward and meet them head on." Tortoise's voice became a forceful zephyr. "Take this moment and push the Iam back into the hole they crawled out of!"

The force of Grandfather Tortoise's speech pushed Joonie back on his heels. "Rabbit, the powers that put you and the Iam here now play a dangerous game. Fate pushes you toward this fight, but you still have to make a choice. Everything depends on that choice." The fight had left Grandfather Tortoise as he struggled to get the last few words out.

"What?" asked Joonie, perplexed.

The Watchi expanded its orbit as the withered shell it circled grew still and became a permanent part of the prairie.

Grandfather Tortoise closed his eye and slowly released his final breath. "Goodbye, Brother Runner," he told Joonie.

The Watchi left the lifeless husk of Grandfather Tortoise, gravitated toward Joonie, and, in its smallest form, began to circle him.

♦

As Joonie's mind raced with what choice he had to make, the Watchi buzzed about him in a spastic flight, bumbling off his ears and face. Joonie swatted at it, but it avoided him expertly. The more agitated Joonie grew, the more agitated the Watchi stone became. Joonie stumbled toward Pencilthin and Bedbug, madly trying to wave away the orbiting stone.

"Calm down, Joonie," Bedbug implored.

"How can I with this whatchacallit stone bouncing off my head?"

Bedbug calmly repeated herself. "Joonie, you need to calm down. The Watchi Stone reflects your state of mind."

Joonie fell to the ground and closed his eyes, digging his paws into the earth and drawing his breath up from the pads of his paws. As he exhaled, he cleared his mind. The Watchi returned to a gentle orbit around Joonie.

"Make it smash that boulder," commanded Pencilthin.

Joonie opened one eye and glared at the porcupine. "Give me a second here, Pencilthin. I'm pretty sure Grandfather Tortoise had a little more time to practice that trick."

Pencilthin shrugged.

Joonie sat for a moment processing all that Grandfather Tortoise had said. *A choice?* He thought back to the mesa top and wondered if he had already made the choice when he accepted being the Runner. *If everything goes according to plan, I won't even see the Iam, let alone have to face them in battle. They'll be turned back by the bison at the edge of the canyon and finished off by the predators.*

Joonie knew in his gut that the quickly hatched plan was a long shot. He knew nothing of the Iam and what they were capable of. *I should have asked him about the Iam. All I wanted to know is if there was any way to get out of this mess. I wasted my question.* The Watchi orbited him erratically, wobbling with every thought that passed through Joonie's head.

Pencilthin and Bedbug saw Joonie's confidence leaving him.

The Watchi, now a sheepish pale yellow, was in a slow orbit near Joonie's tail.

Bedbug approached him. "What did Grandfather Tortoise say?" she asked.

"A lot of stuff that confused me," Joonie replied.

"Well, what did he say about the Iam?"

"He said I was going to have to make a choice, and that a lot of unseen forces had conspired to set the stage for this battle. He said I needed to push forward and face the Iam head on."

Pencilthin had joined the two rabbits. "Well then, what are we waiting for? If Grandfather Tortoise says meet the Iam head on, let's go do it!"

The porcupine's confidence penetrated Joonie's despondence. "You're right, Pencilthin! Everything is in motion. Let's go out to the southern rim and watch these events unfold." The Watchi collected in a tight orbit in front of Joonie.

"Let's move out!" shouted Bedbug above the din of the oncoming stampede.

Together they headed away from the Confluence and toward the impending battle.

CHAPTER TWELVE

The Bridge

The dust whipped across the prairie with enough force to strip bark from the trees. Joonie, Pencilthin, and Bedbug bent into the wind, slowly marching toward the south rim. The noise from the Harbinger Stampede was deafening. The trio could not open their eyes for fear of being blinded, and they could not hear each other over the din of the stampede. Still, the trio pushed forward into the dust cloud and toward the vicious Iam.

After walking for hours in those brutal conditions, they stopped and took refuge behind a large rock outcropping. While they enjoyed a slight reprieve from the horrendous winds and dust, the noise of the stampede made it impossible to communicate with each other. The three of them were alone with their thoughts, each trying to comprehend the fear and panic of the bison.

Instead of speaking, Pencilthin took a quill from his back and drew a simple map in the settled dust. It was a chart showing their position, which, according to the porcupine, was very near the south rim of Cobre Canyon. They all nodded in agreement: They would stay put until the bison turned and headed north again.

♦

On the north side of the canyon, the bison charged headlong south with no sign of slowing down. The Wadi were so vicious in their chase, they began clubbing down the slower bison. The bison ran toward the canyon rim, out of their minds with fear. The Alooshi maintained their sentry around the perimeter, constantly taking large steps inward and shrinking the width of the stampede. Thousands of more bison died of exhaustion and suffocation. The animals were so tightly packed the dead were carried along between them.

♦

As Joonie had hoped and Goyo and Grub had facilitated, the predators gathered farther north. Thousands of mountain lions, coyotes, badgers, wolverines, and foxes shared information about the power shift amongst predator and prey. Magpies, ravens, and crows circled above the group, cawing loudly. The news had spread that the prey had learned to defeat the predators. The hunters blamed the Iam for teaching the hunted to become the hunters. None amongst them were willing to let this shift happen without a fight.

Grub yelled above the roar of the wind. "Predators! Our position at the top of the food chain is being threatened. The prey has figured out how to kill us!"

The predators screeched and howled against the idea.

"The creatures who are new to the surface have taught them to betray their instincts and act like us!"

More barks and hisses were heard from the gathered crowd.

"We are gathered here because a little bunny has challenged us to a fight." Laughter erupted from the crowd. "This little bunny and his porcupine friend have killed two hawks and a coyote!"

The group grew quiet. A snide fox shouted, "And stood on your snout, Grub!"

Grub's band barked at the fox. Suddenly, though, they were drowned out by a tremendous roar. The sound sent cold shivers down the backs of all who had gathered.

Standing tall in the back of the group were the grizzly bears. Together they roared again, bringing the crowd to full attention.

"The Iam will die, and the prey will be reminded of their place!" growled the largest of the bears.

The predators joined in a bloodcurdling battle cry.

Miles away, the Overseer stopped and looked north toward the sound.

♦

The first bison fell over the north rim and tumbled like a sack of corn down the thousand-foot wall, landing with a splat on the canyon floor. Driven by fear and panic, the subsequent bison hurled themselves into the canyon by the thousands. The canyon floor was soon covered in growing layers of dead bison. They slowly began filling the canyon with their carcasses.

♦

On the opposite side of the canyon, Joonie felt deep terror in the pit of his stomach. He left the security of the rock outcropping where he sought shelter with Pencilthin and Bedbug and began to slowly approach the south rim.

The wind had died down, leaving Joonie able to hear the cries and groans of the bison as they launched into the abyss. He saw on the far side of the canyon a black tide tumbling over the canyon wall. *It's like a waterfall*, he thought, trying to wrap his head around the brutal enormity of this genocide.

Pencilthin and Bedbug joined Joonie. They held hands, eyes wide in horror, as they watched the corpses of thousands of bison begin to fill up the canyon. All three animals became hypnotized by the slaughter. They were rooted in place by a feeling of helplessness. At one point Bedbug raised a paw toward the far canyon wall as if to stem the tide of bison falling into the canyon. Her paw seemed so small against the backdrop of careening bison that she returned it to her side.

Pencilthin was the first to shake from the sickening stupor. He knew he and his friends needed an escape from the noise and violence but there was no escape. The entire prairie was engulfed in the noise of the slaughter. Pencilthin led Joonie and Bedbug behind a small berm that had been formed over the years by the wind. Together they burrowed a den and took shelter in its darkness.

Bedbug leaned against the newly dug wall and immediately jumped up and scampered about frantically. "Where's my trace?" she cried, looking about for the bouncing bunnies of the Bedbug trace.

"They are at the Confluence with Grey," Pencilthin said, placing a gentle paw on Bedbug. "They are safe."

Bedbug huddled closely to Joonie and carefully next to Pencilthin. They sat in the damp darkness of the den trying to shut out the noise of the stampede.

After a long silence, Bedbug asked Joonie, "What do you know of the Iam?"

"It's so strange," Joonie began. "When Father Sun would tell me the stories of the Runners and Iam, it was as if he were making it up as he went along. I imagined the Runners to be strong warriors who faced the Iam with might and force. Certainly not a tortoise, or a rabbit for that matter." Joonie took a moment, taking in the damp smell of the hole and remembering the stories Father Sun told. "I remember one thing Father Sun told me that I never understood. He said, 'The Iam is the shadow of the Runner.'"

Pencilthin let out a nervous laugh in the darkness. "What is that supposed to mean?"

"I have no clue," Joonie said simply.

♦

Worn out and driven mad by days of nonstop running, the bison had reached the end of their journey: a thousand-foot plunge to the bottom of Cobre Canyon.

After hours of sitting in the burrowed hole, the trio returned to the southern rim of the canyon. What they saw was even more horrifying than what they'd already witnessed.

As the canyon began to fill with carcasses, the fall was no longer great enough to kill the new bison that hurtled over the north rim. The injured beasts endured torture and agony as hundreds of their brethren landed on top of them, suffocating them. The threesome squeezed each other's hands, rage boiling up through them as they witnessed the most horrific act of violence ever seen in the Front Range.

Eventually the number of living bison began to decrease. The din of the stampede also decreased, leaving the trio able to hear the war cry of the Wadi. The dust storm returned, obscuring the canyon as it echoed with the moaning and thrashing of the dying bison.

Soon the entire canyon was erased from sight by dust. The wind whipped and howled and then died. The prairie was left in complete silence. No more stampeding, no more war screams. Just dust and emptiness.

Joonie, still holding the hands of his friends, took a deep breath. He felt his pulse pounding in his throat. Rage, controlled by careful breathing, continued to grow in the pit of Joonie's stomach. The Watchi Stone circled closely in a forceful orbit.

The dust began to settle. Joonie wiped his eyes and tried to focus. He could not, would not, comprehend the evil that would drive living creatures to their deaths by the thousands.

♦

With the dust settling, the Overseer finally was able to see what was happening on the south side of the canyon. His eyes were immediately drawn to confluence where the rising smoke oppressed under the temperature inversion.

"The signal," he whispered.

Turning toward the lines of Iam, the Overseer spoke. "The sheep has sent the signal. The Runner is near the Confluence. Now is the time of the Iam!"

♦

Joonie could also see clearly now. His eyes able to pick out a red cloak and white mask on the north side of the canyon. Behind the cloak was the blur of a thousand creatures swinging clubs wildly in the air.

Joonie's pulse quickened. He watched the figure in the red cloak begin to walk. At first it seemed like he was walking across the empty, dust-filled air of the canyon. Then it became clear. He was walking on a carpet of fur, of meat, of bone and agony.

"They made a bridge," Bedbug said, her eyes wide in disbelief. "A bridge out of bison."

♦

When the dust settled, the ravens flew south, finally able to see through the obscurity of the cloud. What they saw sent them back to the predators in a panic.

"They drove the bison to their death," said Mal, deeply shaken by what he witnessed.

"What happened?" asked Grub.

"The Iam filled the canyon with bison they drove over the edge. And now they're walking across their dead flesh to the other side."

More reports began to arrive sharing the same gruesome news about the bison genocide.

"Did you see the rabbit?" Grub asked Mal.

"Yes, from a distance. He and two others were standing on the southern rim."

The bunny did not expect this, Grub thought. *Who could have imagined that the Iam were capable of using an entire family of animals for such a reason?* He began to realize the fight the predators needed to fight was not with the prey. It was with the Iam.

He turned to the gathered predators. "The Iam have driven all the bison into the canyon!" he yelled for all to hear. There was shuffling and grunts of anguish and disbelief from the predators. "The Iam have eliminated the bison," he said, pointing toward the destroyed prairie, "and all the animals that once lived on these grasslands. They have taken away our food source! They have taken away our way of life! They will not stop until all the land is left a desert wasteland. We must rid the surface of them!"

The bears roared. The mountain lions hissed. United in self-preservation and vengeance, they charged south after the Iam.

♦

Joonie turned his head from the carnage in the canyon and looked behind him at the beautiful grassland, a sea of soft green and yellow dotted with bushes and filled with boroughs and dens. Then he looked back across the bison-filled canyon at the brown, lifeless desert beyond.

The Watchi Stone orbited Joonie in a slow, powerful orbit, as if passing through the dense energy of rage that was emanating from the rabbit.

Tears of sorrow and rage filled his eyes. Joonie drew a breath from beneath his feet, pulled it up from the earth itself. He released it in a roar as he charged toward the figure in the red cloak that was flanked by Alooshi. Chest out, head held high, Joonie breathed in and out slowly, never taking his eyes of the cloak.

His stride expanded. The Alooshi could not see the approach of this small, furry animal charging across the prairie on to the backs of the struggling bison. But the Overseer could. Clutching his red cloak, he watched as the rabbit gained speed but held steady his position.

The Watchi was now the size of Joonie's head, pulsing red and gold. It buzzed with energy.

The Runner, thought the Overseer.

The Alooshi's attention, however, was drawn away to the Southern Rim, where some activity was brewing. They were oblivious to the charging rabbit.

As Joonie bounded over the broken bodies of the bison, he began to feel weak and sick. The power that he had learned to draw up from the earth through his paws was being sucked out of him. Atop the carnage he could feel buried bison struggling for breath underneath him. Joonie collapsed on top of a dying bison. He felt the faint breath of a beast and looked into his large golden eye, which reflected Joonie's image. Small and weak. From the corner of the bison's mouth hung his tongue, a dusty white muscle dried out from the panicked journey of the stampede.

The Overseer watched as the Runner collapsed. To use the bison for a bridge was only a part of the plan. The Overseer also knew that Runners draw their power from the earth. A canyon filled with death and murder would stop them dead in their tracks.

Joonie felt himself sliding between the bodies of the bison. The Watchi was being drawn down into the murderous heap. As Joonie's head became almost buried, he saw the figure in the red cloak, hidden behind his mask, wave his arms commanding the Iam to press forward. The Alooshi and Wadi surrouned the Overseer.

Joonie inhaled the dying breath of the bison. Unable to move he surrendered, the Watchi stone now gone from him. Joonie closed his eyes.

♦

Joonie recognized the teasing tone of Ghost Cat.

"Runners run, rabbit. Rabbits burrow. Which are you?"

"A Runner?" he responded weakly.

Joonie looked up into the emerald green eyes of his predator. Ghost Cat licked her powerful paw and rubbed it across her face. In a flash she reared back her paw, claws extended. "Damn right you are!" She swiped toward Joonie who blew out his remaining breath and inhaled deeply. Ghost Cat dissipated as Joonie took her in.

Joonie was charged with the power of the big cat. He was now a small rabbit filled with the agility and strength of a mountain lion. He emerged from the pile of dying bison, ready to pounce on the figure in the red cloak.

The Overseer was surrounded by hundreds of Iam as he made his way across the bison bridge toward the southern rim. The Wadi clubbed any bison still struggling. Bedbug and Pencilthin carefully picked their way across the bridge whispering prayers of safe passage to the bison.

The Wadi saw the two small creatures and charged toward them, swinging their clubs wildly. The Alooshi approached in a line, their chains ready for attack.

The bridge began to shift as if it had been hit by an earthquake. The Iam slowed their progress as they tried to remain standing. The bridge rumbled again tossing some Iam about.

The Overseer and the surrounding phalanx retreated back to the north rim.

"The bison are still settling. We will cross soon."

Joonie, filled with the strength of Ghost Cat, charged after them.

As the Overseer reached the north rim, the bison bridge began to undulate and boil with movement. The Iam unit moved away from the canyon and regrouped. They watched as the Iam that remained on the bridge were buried and smashed between the mighty carcasses. Joonie bounded over the unsteady terrain, focused solely on the figure in red.

"Be ready," the Overseer shouted. "The Runner approaches!"

The Wadi and Alooshi on the north rim steadied themselves and swung their weapons.

As soon as Joonie jumped off the back of a dead bison and

landed on terra firma, the Iam charged toward him. Joonie, one small bunny, ran full speed toward hundreds of Iam wielding clubs and chains.

The Overseer braced for the battle.

Joonie jumped toward the first club-wielding Wadi. The Wadi took a stance and swung the club full force, hitting Joonie squarely in the body and sending him flying toward the rim of the canyon.

Joonie tumbled breathlessly toward the rim. His head swam in warm colors as a dark cloud of unconsciousness threatened to overtake him. He felt as if his bones were splintered. Joonie fought hard not to pass out. He heard the laughter of the Iam.

"Hurry and finish him!" he heard the Overseer shout from behind the expressionless white mask.

The Iam rushed toward Joonie, intent on smashing him into the ground.

From deep beneath the bison bridge, another tremor erupted.

Come on, get up! Joonie forced himself to his feet. Following Grandfather Tortoise's instruction, he regained his footing and charged forward, meeting the Iam head on. Behind him the canyon of bison roiled.

The Iam charged toward Joonie.

Bursting from the pits of Cobre canyon came Joonie's Watchi Stone followed by thousands of bison who had not been killed in the fall. The bison hit the ground running toward the Wadi and Alooshi. They lowered their mighty heads and plowed into them, horns first.

The first lines of Iam were trampled into the prairie.

Joonie and the Watchi stone followed close behind the charging bison. He focused on the figure in the red cloak being protected by Wadi. Joonie hopped on the back of a bison and charged toward the group. The Wadi lifted their clubs in anticipation. Joonie focused his attention on the front line of Wadi. The Watchi Stone, sent by Joonie's intentions, flew into the wall of Iam surrounding the Overseer. The stone surrounded the Wadi in a radiant light, paralyzing them. As the light intensified, the Wadi began to bloat. They grew fatter and fatter as the light became more radiant until, in an instant, a blinding bright light flashed.

All the Wadi within it exploded.

Joonie and the bison he rode were temporarily blinded by the light. His steed stumbled, pitching Joonie forward. He flew through the air toward the Overseer. Seizing the momentum provided by the bison stumble, he hauled back and uncorked a punch in the face of the Overseer that sent the white mask flying and its wearer tumbling.

Joonie reeled around. *Wow,* he thought. *I knocked him out cold.* Then he looked at the unmasked face of the Overseer. *Wait... her?*

A thin trickle of blood ran down the fair skin of the Overseer. Her face was the most beautiful thing Joonie had ever seen.

Just then Joonie heard the war whoops from more ranks of Wadi. Reluctantly he looked away from the Overseer and saw a thousand Wadi swinging clubs, beating down the charging bison and heading straight for him.

As they approached, he surrendered to his fate and braced for impact. He looked once more at the beautiful face of the Overseer and then south to see if he could spot his friends. They were sure to share the same painful death as him.

Joonie blinked. It looked as though the grasslands beyond were flowing like a river.

Bounding across the bison bridge was the Red Earth Trace.

Hundreds of thousands of rabbits charged across the plain. Betraying their instinct to run and hide, they pushed forward, each accompanied by a Ghost Predator. The land was filled with fox-rabbits and badger-rabbits, snake-rabbits and coyote-rabbits. Their collective war whoop sent chills through Joonie.

The Trace moved in perfect harmony as it attacked the Wadi. Tens of thousands of Rabbits covered the first line of Wadi like a wave breaking on the shore. The rabbits burrowed into the Wadi's mouths and clawed their way through their bodies, leaving them bleeding to death. The Wadi's clubs were useless. The rabbits swarmed up their arms and forced them to the ground. The subsequent phalanxes of Wadi swung widely into the Trace, smashing rabbits by the hundreds, but they were soon overwhelmed by the fury of small bunnies.

Then a dark shadow crossed the battlefield. Joonie saw an enormous black cloud made up of birds of prey. The birds, working in conjunction with the Iam, began to drop like rain, plucking rabbits off the ground and dropping them from great heights like stones of hail. The plummeting rabbits crashed onto the backs of the earthbound rabbits. Within moments, the birds had reduced the Trace to a number that gave the Wadi a chance to swing their clubs in unison, clearing great swaths as they marched forward.

In the midst of the mayhem, Joonie heard the women in the red cloak moan. *The Overseer,* Joonie thought. He began to make his way over to her when a golden eagle swooped down and grabbed Joonie by one of his ears. Joonie looked around him for the Watchi stone, but it had not returned to Joonie since its attack of radiant light. The eagle regained elevation. Joonie kicked and gnashed at the bird, but it swiftly rose above the fray, taking Joonie with him.

Despite his pain and precarious situation high above the battlefield, Joonie looked out across the Front Range which was now a sad harmony of life and death. The northern lands of the valley trampled and lifeless, Cobre Canyon filled with the dead and dying bison, and to the south the still green and diverse prairie landscape that was home to countless animals.

He remembered something Father Sun had said while he lay dreaming in the mouth of the old hole: *The Runners have won many battles against the Iam, but none have won the war.* Joonie recognized that he might be the first Runner not to win the battle.

He imagined the rest of the valley and its inhabitants destroyed. His eyes once again focused on the lifeless valley to the north. In the distance he saw the troop of predators stalking toward the unsuspecting Iam. *Maybe we haven't lost the battle yet*, Joonie thought, regaining his will to fight.

In order to keep his ear from being torn off, Joonie grabbed the talon of the bird and held tightly to it. The bird could no longer drop Joonie onto members of the Red Earth Trace below. Realizing this, the bird began circling a large patch of prickly-pear cactus, intending to drag Joonie through it.

On its first flyover, Joonie's hind legs were dragged through the cactus, which stuck him with hundreds of needles. The tender pads of his feet received the brunt of the impact with the cactus. Joonie, his eyes welling with tears, could no longer see. The pain was like being set on fire. Every small movement drove the needles deeper into his flesh.

The bird circled around for another pass. This time, though, he dropped Joonie lower so that his underbelly and sides bumped over the cactus. The pain was excruciating. As the bird circled for its third pass, Joonie's paw began to slip from the eagle's talon.

Suddenly, the eagle began to fly erratically. Joonie looked up; the sky was filled with a throbbing cloud of flittering feathered maddess. The eagle was being relentlessly pestered by swarms of small, migrating birds. The black cloud of small birds swallowed up the attacking birds of prey like a shadow. The little birds pecking at the eyes, wings and bodies of the more powerful predator birds.

"Hiya, bunny," shouted a tiny wren.

"Ah-ho," said Joonie weakly.

The small birds pecked at the eyes of the eagle, who jerked this way and that to avoid the little pests. The birds harassed the eagle until he could take it could take no more and flew down to return Joonie to the ground.

When Joonie was close enough, he dropped from the eagle's grasp and landed hard on the dirt. The cactus needles were driven by the impact deeper into Joonie's paws. He tried to stand, but the pain was too great. He could not walk and certainly could not run. Tears of pain and frustration streamed down Joonie's face and rolled off his whiskers.

With cactus needles covering most his body, Joonie rolled onto his back and looked into the sky. The swarm of small, migrating birds and birds of prey was a seething cloud of wings and talons. The little birds were being snatched by the larger birds' sharp beaks and thrown to the ground below.

The small birds, Joonie realized, were being driven back toward the Confluence. Again the birds of prey dove and attacked the rabbits.

Carefully raising his head, Joonie watched the Wadi and Alooshi tear through charging rabbits with chains and clubs. The rabbits' numbers were reduced greatly as the Iam crunched across the broken bodies of the bison bridge.

Joonie attempted to raise himself from the prairie floor, but the needles just sank deeper into his flesh. He fell back and closed his eyes, surrendering once more to his fate. He felt the warmth of the Sun on his face.

I didn't even win the battle, father. I didn't even win the battle.

CHAPTER THIRTEEN

Grey

Joonie opened his eyes when he heard the familiar bickering of Eeka and Meeka Mouse.

"Okay, Mister Mystic. What do we do now that the Runner is dead?" It was Eeka.

"This is certainly not good," said Meeka as he watched the Iam storm across the canyon. "Not good at all."

"Hey, guys," whispered Joonie. "A little help here."

Eeka and Meeka jumped and ran toward Joonie.

"We found your little stone," said Eeka, handing Joonie the Watchi. It pulsed a weak light which grew a little stronger in Joonie's presence.

Carefully they began to remove the cactus needles embedded deep in Joonie's flesh.

As they worked, Joonie saw the rabbits and small birds begin to retreat. By the time Joonie could stand again, the Iam were reaching the southern rim of the canyon.

"Have you seen Pencilthin and Bedbug?" asked Joonie.

The mice shook their heads.

"Pencilthin is battling hard Joonie. It doesn't look good for him. I don't know how much more he can take" came the soft voice of Bedbug, limping toward the small group. She was covered in dirt and blood. "He's fighting hard but there are just so many of them."

Eeka and Meeka finished pulling out the last few cactus spines as Joonie, once again gathered strength he didn't know he had, stood up. Bedbug rushed over and lent her paw to assist him. Together, Joonie, the mice, and Bedbug walked toward the hundreds of oncoming Iam. The Overseer had regained consciousness and was leading the hoard.

"What are we doing, Joonie?" asked Bedbug.

"Betraying our instincts," said Joonie.

Meeka followed the pair of rabbits. "Meeka, what do think you're up to?" shouted Eeka.

"Betraying my instincts," mimicked Meeka.

"Oh, hell," sighed Eeka as he chased after them.

♦

The women in the red cloak raised her hand, and the Iam stopped marching south. The Iam took a knee as she alone was the first of the Iam to breach the southern side of the canyon. She approached Joonie, Bedbug, and the mice.

Joonie felt a lump grow in throat as the beautiful woman approached him. The Watchi Stone, still weak from its efforts, betrayed Joonie's enrapture with the Overseer and perked up as she approached.

Bedbug punched Joonie in his ribs. "C'mon, rabbit! Focus!"

Joonie shook himself out of his stupor.

"Settle down, Runner," said the Overseer, gently watching the Watchi's orbit. "What is it about boys? So easily excited." She smiled.

Embarrassed, Joonie tried to control the stone.

"Are you a good rabbit or an evil rabbit?" she asked Joonie simply.

Joonie blinked.

"Or are you just a fool?"

Joonie stammered, thinking of his friends and foes. "I… I guess it depends on who you ask."

"Why are you fighting us? Do you even know? Do even know what you are fighting against?" she asked.

"I..."

"You are a fool, Runner." She laughed and reached down to pick a delicate flower from the pristine south side of the canyon. She lifted it to her face and inhaled its scent. Then she closed her eyes, and her face relaxed.

"Mother did a glorious job on the flowers, don't you think?" she asked Joonie, her eyes still closed.

"Mother?" asked Joonie.

"Just look at it. The perfection of the universe reflected in the pedals. The overwhelming beauty detected by the eyes and the nose. Smell it, Runner." She handed the flower over to Joonie.

Joonie, under the spell of the women in the red cloak, took the flower from her. Bedbug crossed her arms.

"I think I shall name the flower... bergamot," said the Overseer to a nearby Tar-Reef who was ready with a tablet and pen.

Joonie deeply inhaled the scent of the flower. "Bergamot, huh? Yeah, it's nice." He handed the flower to Bedbug, but she kept her arms folded and rolled her eyes.

"Nice," repeated the Overseer, shaking her head. "That is precisely why we are here."

"Speaking of nice, you'd make a nice hat, rabbit," sneered the Tar-Reef peeking from behind the red cloak.

A chill went up Joonie's spine. *Hat?* He thought, *Hat rabbit?* Joonie shook the feeling that he had heard that before and returned his attention to the Overseer. "So, you are here to name the flowers?" asked Joonie.

"You really are a little fool, rabbit. Look around you." She swept her arm across the prairie and towards the snow-capped mountains. Flat-bellied clouds drifted slowly over the Front Range, throwing shadows across the land that moments before was illuminated.

"This is the most exquisite creation in the universe. And you dumb animals don't even recognize it. We are not here for the flowers, Runner. We are here to appreciate Mother's creation. To give her grand design the respect it deserves. We are here to give this a name."

Joonie shuffled his feet, once again not understanding what was being said to him.

"We have come at the request of the Mother. She wants her work acknowledged and appreciated," the Overseer said at last.

"Mother Moon sent you?"

"No, not Mother Moon. Mother Earth." She smirked. "Mother Moon and Father Sun would rather that we never arrive. That is why they raised you and all the Runners before you. To keep Mother Earth unappreciated."

Joonie was stunned. He had always imagined Mother Earth as kindly and nurturing.

The Overseer had collected a bouquet of prairie flowers and began to place them in her flowing hair. Her graceful fingers weaved the stems delicately. Her eyes closed when she inhaled their fragrance. Joonie had never seen anyone more at peace than the Overseer.

Joonie became aware of his nervous shuffling and stopped. He soon started rocking back and forth, trying to find something to appreciate even half as much as the Overseer appreciated those flowers. *The mountains are pretty,* he thought, not knowing if he truly appreciated them.

"The runners cannot keep the Mother Earth from being worshiped. It is what she desires most."

"Why would Mother Moon and Father Sun want to keep

Mother Earth from being worshiped?" After a little more thought he asked, "And how does forcing the bison into the canyon and trampling the prairie equal appreciation?"

Eeka and Meeka nodded.

"Because, rabbit, even beyond the supreme power of Mother Earth there is something far more powerful that controls the universe."

"What is it?"

"Comedy," the Overseer said.

"Comedy? I don't see how this is funny."

"What's funny is that Mother Earth desires nothing more than for her creation to be recognized and appreciated. Who can blame her? Behold the color of the sky, the reciprocal prowess of the clouds, the sheer efficiency of her systems." The Overseer's eyes gleamed with admiration. "Her work is so magnificent." She stopped and slowly bowed her head. "Lifetimes could be spent contemplating her simplest creation."

Joonie observed a slow moving cloud drift by. *Wow, this is pretty, I guess,* he thought. *I never really thought of the land as something to be admired.* A warm breeze blew the tall grasses, and

Joonie caught a whiff of the bergamot followed by the grotesque hint of decay coming from the canyon. *I still don't get what's so funny.*

As if reading his mind, the Overseer continued "The comedy is inescapable," she said, staring directly into Joonie's eyes. Then she pointed at the clouds and mountains on the horizon. "The sad fact is, for something to be this magnificent, something else must be this horrific." She gestured toward the canyon full of dead and dying bison. "There is no beauty without ugliness. There must be this massacre to have that prairie. All this ugliness and hate, all this murder, is what makes love and beauty possible." Then she laughed.

"Why are you laughing?" Joonie asked. "What's so funny?" He stomped his paw.

When the Overseer returned her attention to Joonie, he saw she had tears in her eyes.

"I'm not laughing because something is funny," she said gently. "I'm laughing at how perfectly in balance everything is and always will be. That is what's so funny, Runner. Everything is always exactly right. It can be no other way. And yet, we all rally and get excited, running around trying to change something that cannot be changed. It's hilarious!" She shouted, and her eyes became wild. "It's perfectly hilarious!"

Her laugh made Joonie's spine tingle. The Overseer grew suddenly quiet, her laughter echoing and dying on the wind. The placid expression on her face was replaced by a visage of fear. She wrung her hands. Suddenly she looked frightened. She backed away from Joonie and fell to her knees, sobbing.

An intense empathy swept over Joonie. The surrounding Iam, completely unaware that they were being stalked from the north by the predators, dropped to one knee and bowed their heads.

Joonie, directed by timeless forces, left Bedbug's side and walked right up to the crying women. Taking her hands in his paws, he drew a breath and asked in a whisper, "Why are we here again?"

"Again and again and again," she said, weeping, "you are the Runner, and I the Overseer. Forever in perfect, balanced conflict. We have no choice but to play our parts. It is here, on this surface, witnessed by the stars, that the drama unfolds again and again and again. I have been cast as the villain and you the hero. Forever. Without me, there is no you."

The Iam is the shadow of the Runner, Joonie thought.

Her back was to the western mountains. Joonie was so close to the Overseer he could see the grains of pollen on the stamens of the flowers in her hair and the Moon, rising from the Eastern horizon, reflected in her eyes. With his back to the eastern plain, Joonie returned her gaze, and in his eyes she saw the reflection of the Sun setting behind the Western mountains.

The animals and the Iam witnessed the fragile connection between Joonie and the Overseer silently. The first of the dusk stars glimmered in the sky.

"We can end this dance," he whispered and squeezed the Overseer's hand. In that moment the Moon did not continue to rise, and the Sun did not continue to set. The attending stars grew hazy as the bemused animals, and the Iam lost their hold on the ground and slowly started to float. Even the approaching predators became detached from their mission as the world around them became dreamy and light.

"We don't have to be at odds." Joonie said to the Overseer.

"This is our only moment of choice," she said. "Without us two, there is no pain and there is no love. We can stop it now.

We can be together, become one again." Her eyes glowed with the light of the Moon. Her hands began to slip from Joonie's paws. The entire known universe, aware that it's very existence depends on the choice of these two creatures, expanded uncomfortably.

Reluctantly, Joonie broke away from her gaze and glanced at the heaps of dead and dying rabbits and small, migrating birds. He looked past the dead and dying Iam and Alooshi at Cobre Canyon, filled with bison. He saw the lifeless earth that they had trampled during their horrifying journey.

The pain, he thought.

Joonie took another deep breath and smelled wonderful soup, the soup that was lovingly prepared by the prairie animals. His mouth began to water.

That's when a simple thought popped into his head, *I love soup. I really love soup. I love everyone who made it and everything it is made of.*

His heart filled with love. Joonie looked at the Overseer again and saw the enormous strength in her. "You are willing to be the villain so we may know love?" he asked.

"I am," she said.

"You are the true hero," he said, withdrawing his paw from her hand. "I will love you forever."

"And I you," she returned.

Then, in one swift intention, Joonie sent the Watchi stone toward the Overseer. The stone circled the Overseer who surrendered peacefully. As the Watchi stone orbited faster and faster the Overseer began to glow in a beautiful golden light. The flowers, released from her flowing hair, floated airily around her face. She smiled and reached out a hand toward Joonie and said, "Know this Runner: Beyond even comedy is love. Everything but everything is done in the name of love. Joonie, love conquers all."

The golden light grew more radiant until all the prairie animals had to look away. And then she was gone.

The world once again spun as the Sun disappeared behind the mountains.

Kill the Runner.

The Wadi and Alooshi, following the last mandate of the Overseer, screamed and charged toward Joonie and Bedbug.

Bedbug grabbed Joonie, who was still in a daze. The Iam were approaching fast. "Let's run," yelled Bedbug, but Joonie could not move. His eyes were unfocused. Bedbug slapped, pulled, and pushed Joonie, to no avail. She felt the wind from the clubs being swung by the Wadi. *Oh, this is going to hurt.*

"What's with the rabbit?" came the weak voice of Pencilthin, who was limping in front of them. The porcupine looked terrible. His once proud headdress of quills was now patchy and broken. One eye was swollen shut, and it looked as if his forepaw was broken.

"He won't move," she said.

"Of all the times he doesn't run and hide, it has to be now," laughed Pencilthin. "Well, I guess it's time to obey our instincts."

In a ridiculous act of futility, Pencilthin dug his paws in the earth and stuck his sparse backside toward the mass of rapidly approaching Iam.

Just then a loud roar ripped through the prairie, turning the attacking Iam on their heels. The predators had arrived. They attacked with intense fury and ripped into the Iam without mercy. Fangs, claws, and beaks slashed and gnashed. A grizzly bear swung an Aloosh by his chain, clearing out Iam by the dozen. Wolves that had traveled down from the north attacked with a ferocity that made the coyotes look like prairie dogs. The Iam were torn apart where they stood.

Joonie, finally freed from his spell, joined Bedbug and Pencilthin in the fight. Surrounding the three of them with the protection of the Watchi Stone.

The battle did not last long. The predators destroyed the Iam in moments.

♦

After the fighting was over, there was an eerie silence as the Red Earth Trace and other small prairie animals shuffled nervously in the presence of the predators, whose fangs and claws still dripped with the red blood of the Iam.

Goyo settled next to Joonie on the battlefield.

"You should go and take the prairie animals with you," said the raven. "The Iam destroyed the hunting grounds of the predators, and they are hungry."

The predators were stalking around the battlefield, still filled with the animus and rage they channeled to utterly defeat the Iam. A fox, eyes still red with anger, loped behind Bedbug.

Joonie raised his paw.

"You are all invited to eat with us at the Confluence," shouted

Joonie. "We have plenty of food." The predators looked at Joonie and then at each other, closing in on the prey. "Please, let me be perfectly clear. You are all invited to eat *with* us, not eat *us*."

Soon the smell of cooking soup carried across the grassland toward the group. The coyotes lifted their noses, inhaling the savory scent.

A lone wolf approached Joonie and lay down at his feet. "We would be honored to eat *with* you Runner," he said.

The other predators followed his lead, and all laid down. Some even rolled onto their backs.

Joonie, a lone rabbit, reluctantly accepted the recognition, painfully aware of the humor in the situation. The Overseer might have even called this "comedy."

Joonie, hand in hand with Bedbug, led the group to the Confluence where the company of prairie animals was waiting with piles and piles of food.

Yet when the awaiting animals saw the bears, mountain lions, and other predators they began to scatter and hide.

"Ah-ho," called Joonie. "It's okay. We have a kind of truce. The predators are going to eat with us."

"What do mean, a *kind of* truce?" came a voice hidden under the brush. "We'd be more comfortable with a complete truce."

"Okay, it's a complete truce," said Joonie, "Where is Grey?"

The prairie animals emerged from their hiding places cautiously. "He left right after the soup fires were lit," said a ptarmigan. "He said he had played his part and it was time to return to the high country."

The wolf that bowed to Joonie approached. "They set you up," he growled simply.

"Who?"

"Whoever set those fires. The Iam used the smoke to know when you arrived and where you were."

"How do you know this?" asked Joonie incredulously, not believing that Grey would betray the animals of the Front Range.

"One of our spies overheard the Iam talking about it."

Joonie sat down.

"Grey wanted us to give you this," said the ptarmigan, handing Joonie a letter.

Across the envelope in beautiful handwriting was written the word *Runner*

If you are reading this, then you have learned much about the nature of good and evil and can perhaps understand that all of us play our part. I, too, played my part. For every approach of the Iam there is a Runner, and for every Runner there is a Grey. The forces that carried me to the Confluence and set the signal fires are the same forces that sent the Iam through the Earth's crust. The same forces that blew the scent of soup your direction are the same forces that compelled you to battle the Iam. The role the Greys play is not that of the epic hero nor the horrific monster. We are forgotten when the stories of the battles are retold.

Runner, when you think back on the recent events and place me in them, I ask you to consider this. Which was more significant the smoke signal or the soup? As you ponder this you will know the nature of the Greys.

If you want to thank me or throw rock at me you can find me high above the trees.

Love,

Grey

Once again perplexed, Joonie returned the letter to its envelope. He shook his head and dropped it into the dying embers of a soup fire. He took a deep breath and blew onto the coals until the letter caught fire. Joonie watched as the thin strand of smoke twisted up into the sky.

♦

The predator and the prey ate together in peace for weeks, until the prairie began to grow back. On more than one occasion a predator, forced by their truce to eat the foliage that the prey did, was overheard saying, "This ain't food. This is what food *eats*."

But until the chases, boroughs, and dens began to be sustainable once again, the predators refrained from eating the prey.

No one remembers when the first predator killed the first prey after the Great Harbinger Stampede. By then, no one really noticed.

EPILOGUE

When and how a rabbit trace begins has always been passed along through myths. Through stories and ceremony, young rabbits try to wrap their minds around the beginning of their trace.

When telling the story of the Bedbug Trace, the myth begins with, *It all started with two lone rabbits.*

Thank you to each and every one of you. Special thanks to Jason Heller for helping me bring structure to Joonie's story. Thank you to Ravi Zupa for creating such beautiful art. Thank you Mike King for applying your vast talents to the book design. Thank you Michelle for the greatest gifts I have ever received. Thank you to my mom whose courage is that of the greatest hero.

—D.L.

Photo by Mark Sink

A writer in a restauranteur suit, Daniel Landes has published many short stories and even shorter poems. Some of his work has appeared online, but print is where he finds the most satisfaction. Daniel owns two vegetarian restaurants in Denver, Colorado—WaterCourse Foods and City, O' City—as well as a vegan bakery, WaterCourse Bakery.

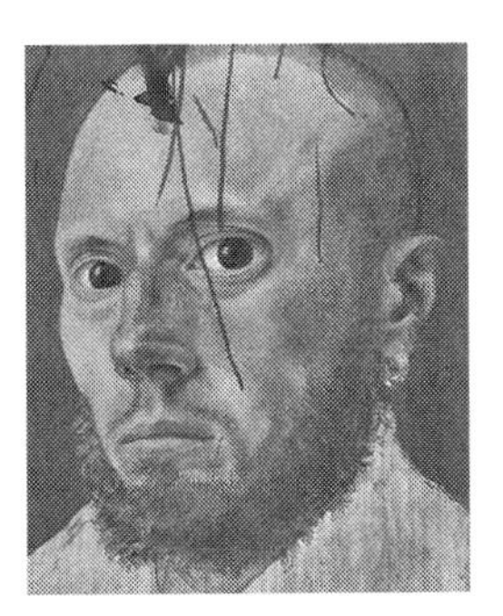

Ravi Zupa's art education started with his family, most notably his mother, and continued at his local library. He has spent the last decade studying art from a wide span of cultures, regions, and history. The art in this book represents the herbivore neighbors around his home in Colorado.